Owl Diaries Collection

Four books in one!
CALL ME

OWL DIARIES

Collection

Rebecca Elliott

BRANCHES™

SCHOLASTIC INC.

ISBN 978-1-338-30587-6

10 9 8 7 6 5 4 3 2 19 20 21 22

Printed in the U.S.A. 23
First printing 2018
Edited by Katie Carella
Book design by Marissa Asuncion

Owl Diaries Collection Table of Contents

OWL DIARIES

BRANCHES™

Eva's Treetop Festival

Rebecca Elliott

SCHOLASTIC

♡ Table of Contents ♡

11
Woodpine Avenue

1 Meet Eva

Tuesday

Hello Diary,

My name is Eva Wingdale. I live at Treehouse 11 on Woodpine Avenue in Treetopolis.

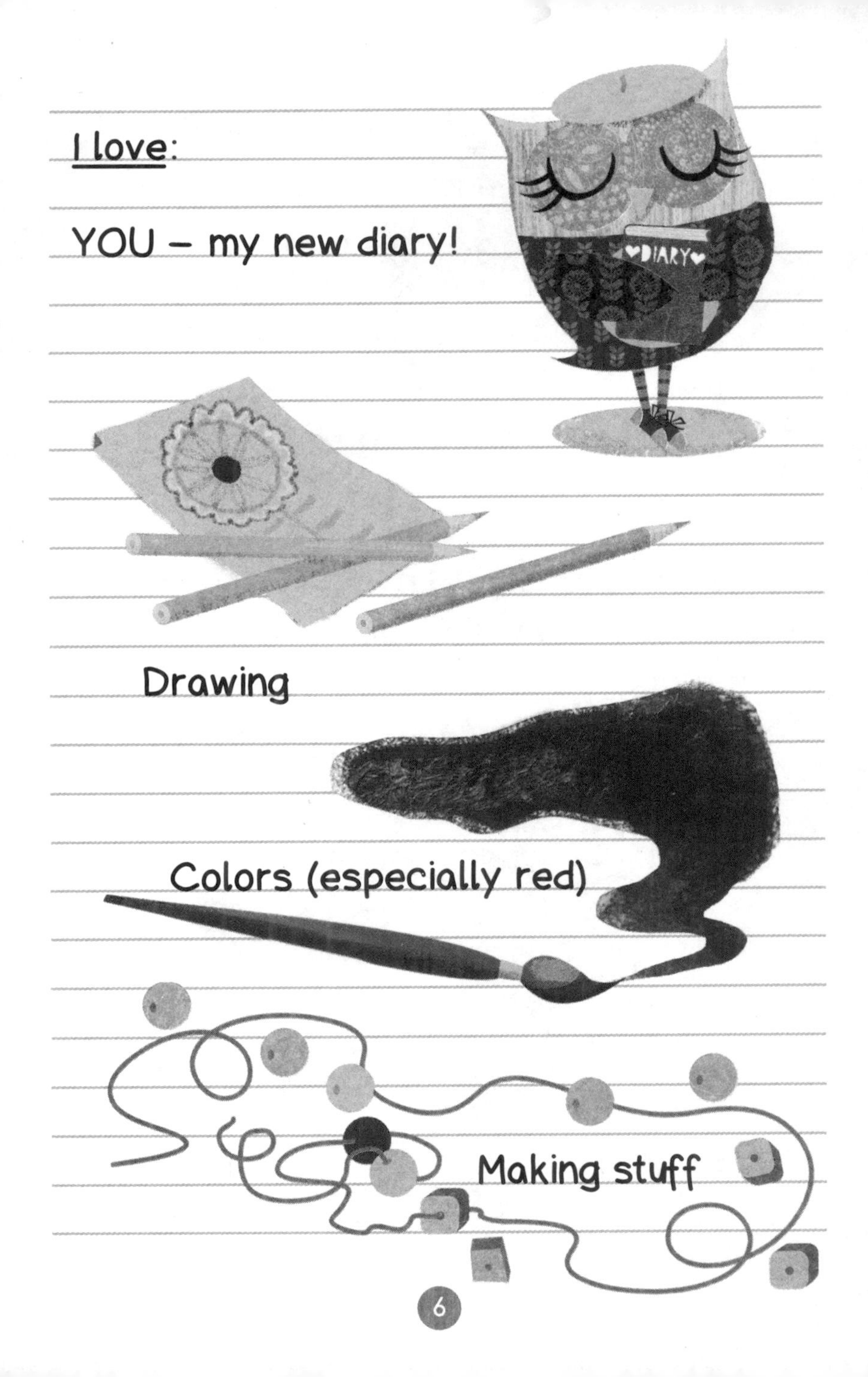
I love:
YOU – my new diary!
♥DIARY♥
Drawing
Colors (especially red)
Making stuff

The word pumpkin

Cool clothes

School

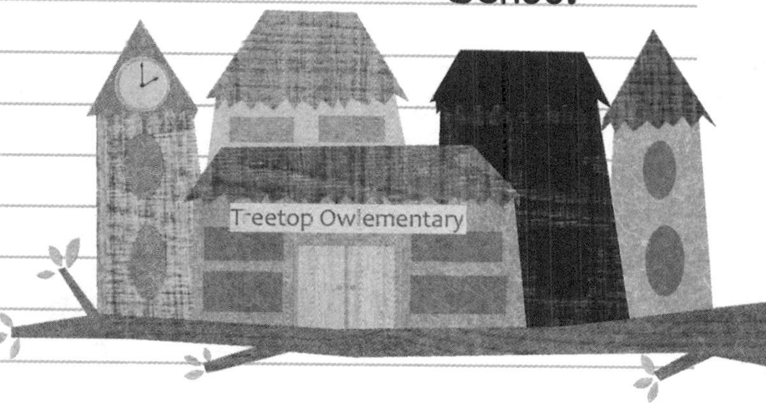
Treetop Owlementary

Being busy

DIARY

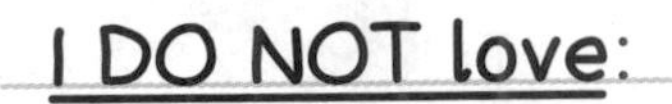

I DO NOT love:

My brother Humphrey's
stinky socks

Sue Clawson
(She is REALLY mean!)

Cleaning my beak

PLOP

The word plop

8+2=?
?

Asking for help

Squirrels

Mom's slug sandwiches

Being bored

Oh, and I'm an owl!

Owls are super cool.

We're awake in the nighttime.

We're asleep in the daytime.

We can turn our heads almost all the way around.

And we can fly!

Here is my owl family:

Me
Dad
the Wingdales
Baby Mo
Humphrey
Mom

AND here is my pet bat, Baxter!

He's so cute!

My very BEST friend in the whole **OWLIVERSE** is Lucy Beakman.

Lucy lives in the tree next door to mine. We have sleepovers all the time!

11
9

Lucy also sits next to me at school. Here is a photo of our class:

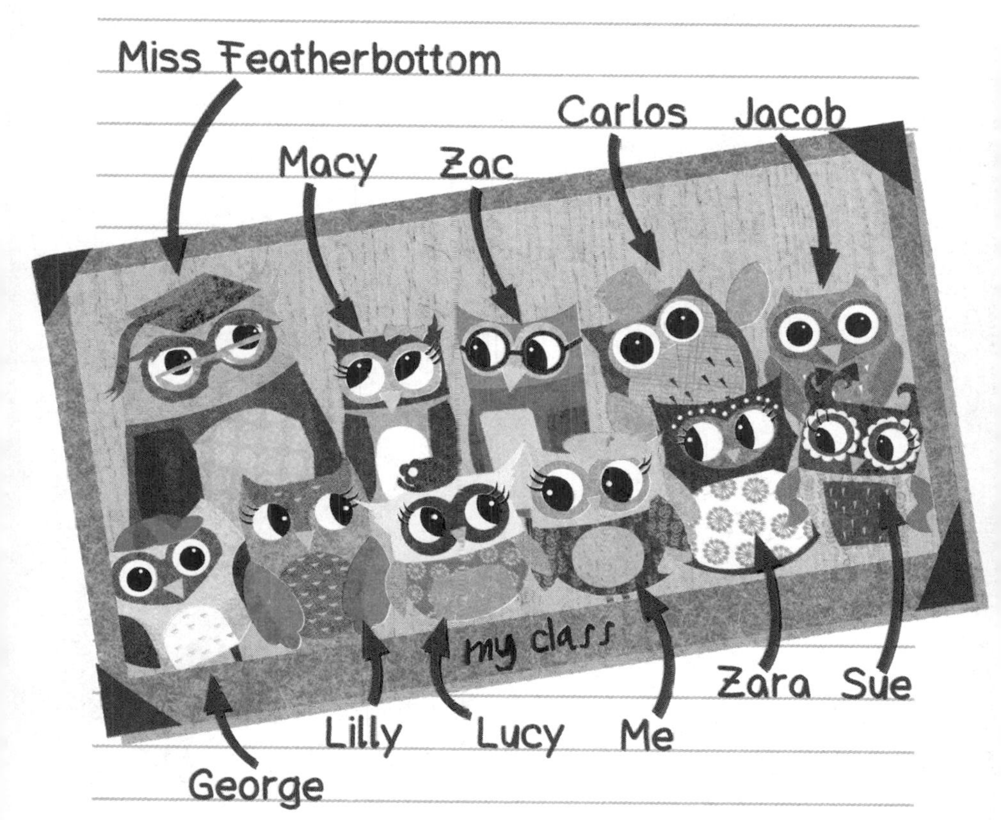

Miss Featherbottom
Macy
Zac
Carlos
Jacob
my class
Zara
Sue
Lilly
Lucy
Me
George

Oh, no! I'm late for school! I'll write again tomorrow, Diary.

Bored, Bored, BORED!

Wednesday

When I got home from school today, I did the same things I always do.

I took Baxter for a fly.

I ate a snack.

I did my **WINGLISH** homework.

I did arts and crafts.

I made this cool bead bracelet!

I tried on new outfits.

I had a fight with Humphrey. He left his stinky socks in my bedroom AGAIN! He is such a squirrel-head!

But after all that, I still had HOURS to go before sunrise. I had <u>nothing</u> to do!

I called Lucy.
Lucy! I am SO bored! Can you come over?
Sorry! I can't. Tomorrow is the first day of spring, so my mom and I are planting flowers.
Flowers? Spring?! Lucy, you are a genius!
Huh? I am? Okay, then!
Gotta go!
Bye, Eva!

Thank goodness for Lucy! She just gave me the most **FLAPPY-FABULOUS** idea!! I need to brainstorm! I'll be back!

Okay, Diary. I've been thinking and thinking. Now I have the BEST plan <u>ever</u>! But there is no time to tell you. I'm off to bed. I cannot wait to tell Lucy (and YOU) all about it tomorrow!

3

Miss Featherbottom

Thursday

Hi Diary,
I told Lucy about my big plan on our flight to school tonight.

Bloomtastic Festival

I am going to organize the first-ever . . . Treetop Owlementary BLOOMTASTIC FESTIVAL!

It's going to be feather-flapping good! There will be fun contests — a talent show, a bake-off, a fashion show, and an art show! And I'll make prizes!

Lucy really liked my idea.

Wow, Eva, that sounds flap-tastic! When will you ask Miss Featherbottom about it?
Tonight. But I'm a bit scared she won't like my idea.

Oh, Eva! She'll LOVE it! It sounds like a lot of work. But it is a great idea!

I went to see Miss Featherbottom, our teacher, as soon as I got to class.

We always celebrate holidays in our classroom, but I was thinking . . . Because today is the first day of spring, our class could have a spring festival! And I'd like to organize it, if that's okay?

Miss Featherbottom didn't say anything. So I kept talking. I told her about the contests and the prizes.

1ST
1ST
1ST
1ST

The festival would be called the Bloomtastic Festival. Because spring is when flowers come out – or, um, bloom. This festival would be ALL about flowers!

Finally, Miss Featherbottom smiled.

A spring festival is a fabulous idea, Eva! What a hoot! And, yes, you may be in charge. But please, dear, don't take on too much yourself. Share the work.

Oh, and the festival can be next Thursday. We will give out your prizes next Friday.

Uh-oh, Diary. Next Thursday is only a week away! How will I get everything done in time?!

But I'm just SO very happy that Miss Featherbottom liked my idea!

YAY!

I told Lucy everything right before class.

Lucy, guess what! Miss Featherbottom loved my idea!
That's flaperrific, Eva!

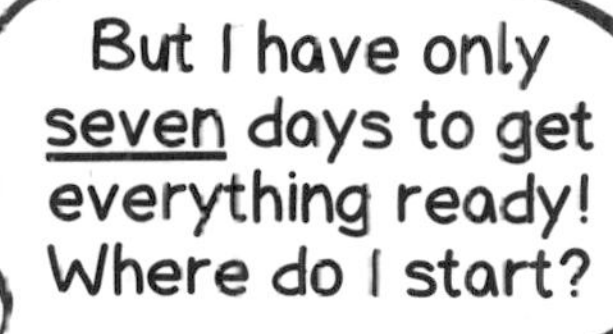
But I have only seven days to get everything ready! Where do I start?

Make a to-do list. Then you'll know what you need to get done.

Lucy is the best friend EVER. She always knows what to do.

As soon as I got home, I wrote my to-do list:

1. Paint the set for the talent show
2. Set up tables for the bake-off
3. Hang frames for the art show
4. Build the runway for the fashion show
5. Make prizes
1ST
1ST
1ST
1ST

This is a great, long list! I know one thing, Diary: I won't be bored anymore! YAY! I'm off to sleep now. Good day!

4

Meany McMeanerson

Friday

Tonight was NOT a good night.

First, Miss Featherbottom told our class about the festival.

The Bloomtastic Festival will be next Thursday! There will be four contests for you to enter. And I will be giving out prizes next Friday.

Then she asked me to come up front. I was a bit nervous as I flew up there.

I told everyone how the festival is all about flowers. Then I told them where to sign up for the contests.

Everything was going well.

Awesome!
Great idea, Eva!

BUT THEN, Sue Clawson said something really bossy.

Why are YOU in charge, Eva?
Who made you festival queen?

My wings got all shaky. Everyone was looking at me. I did not like it.

I'm in charge of the festival because . . . uh . . . it was my idea. And I want everyone to have fun. I don't want anyone else to have to worry about getting things ready.

Well, I should be in charge of the fashion show. My mom is a fashion designer!

I've got that taken care of. But thank you, Sue.

I flew back to my seat.

Sue is always sticking her beak into my business. And she is always SO mean. Her name <u>should be</u> Meany McMeanerson.

MEANY
McMEANERSON
100555

One time Sue told me my mom makes stinky sandwiches. (This is true, but she still shouldn't have said it.)

Then Miss Featherbottom stood up.

Settle down, everyone. I'm sure Eva will ask for some help. And I want you all to have Sue's excellent, helpful attitude! You're setting a wonderful example, Sue. Thank you.

After I organize this amazing festival, I hope Miss Featherbottom will say something nice like that about me, too.

Wait, Diary! My night got even worse after that! Sue walked over to me at lunch.

Good luck building the runway on your own, Eva. You're going to need it!

Argh! Meany McMeanerson is <u>such</u> a meany!

Before bed, I tried not to think about what Sue had said. I'm sure I can build a great runway. Right, Diary?

Now I'm worrying about everything I have to do for the festival. This will be a busy weekend!

Sleep tight, Diary!

5 ♡ Practice Makes Perfect ♡

Saturday

Today, I started to paint the talent show set.

Lucy came over to keep me company — and to work on her contest entries. Since I am planning the festival, I won't be entering the contests. So I wanted to help Lucy!

I gave her my yummiest cupcake recipe for the bake-off.

Eva's Scrummy Cupcakes
1 cup birdseed
1 cup flour
1 cup acorns
2 slugs
- Mix everything together
- Bake for 20 minutes
- Let cupcakes cool
- Put loads of icing on top
- Enjoy!

I promised to help her bake after school on Wednesday. That way, her cupcakes will be super-fresh for Thursday's contest.

Next, I helped Lucy choose an outfit for the fashion show.

Then she painted a picture of her pet lizard, Rex, for the art show. That was such a **HOOT**!

I drew a picture of Baxter wearing a bunny costume, too.

Just before bed, I helped Lucy practice some dance moves for the talent show.

Baxter really liked our moves!

Humphrey did not.

Ha! You two look like a couple of crazy flamingoes doing the cha-cha!

He is such a squirrel-head.

I didn't finish painting the set today. But I have all day tomorrow. So don't worry, Diary. **ANYHOOT**, this festival is going to be great!

6 Time Flies!

Sunday

Hi Diary,

I'm awake super-early!

I haven't finished the talent show set yet, but I want to start building the runway today. (I'll show Sue that I can do this on my own!)

I also have to make the prizes for the festival – they're going to be SO amazing!

Eva!

Uh-oh. Mom's calling me. I'll be back, Diary.

I'm back!

Humphrey and I spent the night with Granny Owlberta and Grandpa Owlfred!

Granny
Grandpa

It was great to see them. But it's almost daytime already! I haven't gotten anything done! EEK! And now the phone is ringing!

Lucy called to see how I'm doing with my to-do list.

Not great, Lucy! I've just been so busy!
Feathering flaps, Eva! The Bloomtastic Festival is only four days away! Are you sure you don't want any help?
Thanks, Lucy, but I still think I'll be okay.

Time flew this weekend! Sorry I can't write more, Diary. But I have to make the prizes before bed. Gotta fly! Bye!

Chapter 7: Too-Hoo Much to Do

Monday

Arrrghhhhhhh!!!

The festival is only THREE DAYS AWAY!

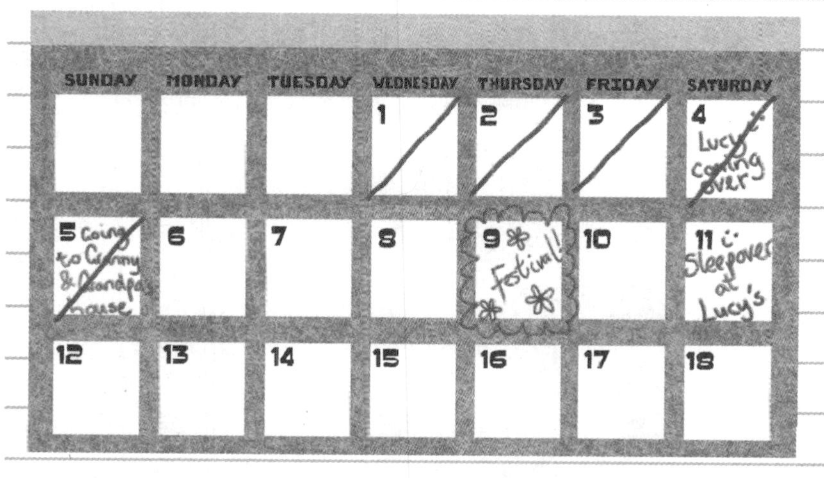
SUNDAY
MONDAY
TUESDAY
WEDNESDAY
THURSDAY
FRIDAY
SATURDAY
1
2
3
4
Lucy coming over
5
6
7
8
9
Festival!
10
11
Sleepover at Lucy's
12
13
14
15
16
17
18

I've been so busy helping Lucy and creating the best prizes EVER that nothing else is ready! (But the prizes are finished. And I can't wait for everyone to see how cool they look!)

Diary, you know I wanted to do this festival all on my own. But I need some help – a LOT of help.

I'm going to talk to Lucy after school. I'll write more later!

Lucy was a BIG help. Well, sort of.

We painted half of the talent show set. But our wings got tired.

We tried to hang the frames for the art show. But we couldn't reach!

We planned a flower-shaped table design for the bake-off. But we didn't start building the table.

We even started building the runway. But it's a really big job!

So we have A LOT left to do:

1. Finish painting the talent show set
2. Hang the frames for the art show
3. Build the flower-shaped table for the bake-off
4. Finish building the runway for the fashion show

Lucy, I just don't have enough wings to do everything.
Don't worry, Eva. We'll figure something out.

Oh, Diary! Will I have to cancel the festival?

8 A Helping Wing

Tuesday

When I woke up today, I thought about how sad everyone would be if we cancelled the festival.

Then I thought about what Miss Featherbottom had said when I first told her my idea.

Share the work!

Finally, Diary! I know what I have to do! I was so silly to think that I could do ALL of this work on my own. NO ONE could! There are so many talented owls in my class. I just have to ask for help! Wish me luck, Diary! I'll write again after school.

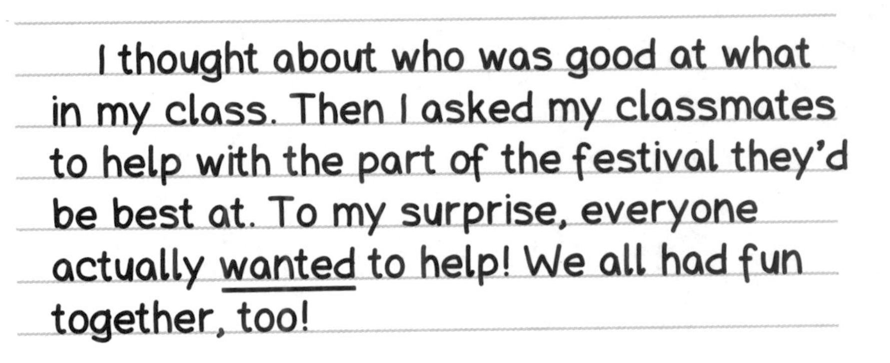

I thought about who was good at what in my class. Then I asked my classmates to help with the part of the festival they'd be best at. To my surprise, everyone actually wanted to help! We all had fun together, too!

George, Carlos, and Zara are the best painters in the class. So I asked them to paint the talent show set.

Zac and Macy are the tallest owls in the class. So I asked them to hang the frames for the art show.

Lilly and Jacob are good at building things. So I asked them to make the table for the bake-off. They loved Lucy's and my flower design!

I still need help with the runway. But Sue was out today. (She had to go to the **OWLADONTIST**!) I must ask for her help tomorrow. But I'm SO nervous.

Lucy, I'm scared of asking Sue for help. What if she laughs at me? What if she says something mean? Or what if she says no?

There's no way to know what Sue will say. Just be the lovely, fluffy, hoot of an owlet that you are and see what happens.

But tomorrow is the day before the festival. If Sue says no and the runway is not ready, we'll have to cancel the fashion show!!!!

9 An Odd Day

Wednesday

I spoke to SUE!! Here is what happened:

Um . . . Sue?
Yeah?
I was just wondering if you might want to help –
Help build the runway?
Yes. Would that be okay?
Of course! I was hoping you'd ask me for help!

I could not believe that Sue said yes. She even smiled at me. Kind of.

Then she helped me build the runway after school.

Later, Lucy came over. We baked her cupcakes for the bake-off contest. And we made a flower on top of each cupcake!

After we made flower cupcakes, we had a flour fight! It was really fun!

It's been an odd day. But a good one. And I cannot believe that TOMORROW is the BIG day, Diary!! EEK!

10

♡ The Festival ♡

Thursday

Hello Diary,
Today's festival was a huge success for everyone . . .

Bloomtastic
Festival!

Just not for me. I spent the day running around to make sure everything was going okay. But everything went wrong.

First, Lucy's cupcakes did not look like pretty flowers. We had frosted the cupcakes when they were still hot. The frosting melted. And now they looked like gloopy SNOT balls!

Next, I saw that my just-for-fun painting of Baxter had been hung up in the art show! Lucy's was nowhere to be seen. She must've turned in my painting by mistake. Oh, Lucy! No one was supposed to see mine! Baxter looked like a <u>CRAZY ALIEN!</u>

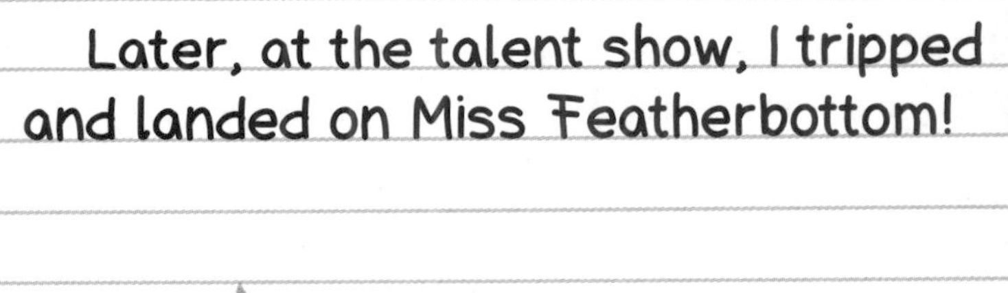
Later, at the talent show, I tripped and landed on Miss Featherbottom!

Um. Hope you're enjoying the show!

The fashion show was the last contest. And I walked out onstage with my dress tucked into my <u>underpants</u>!!

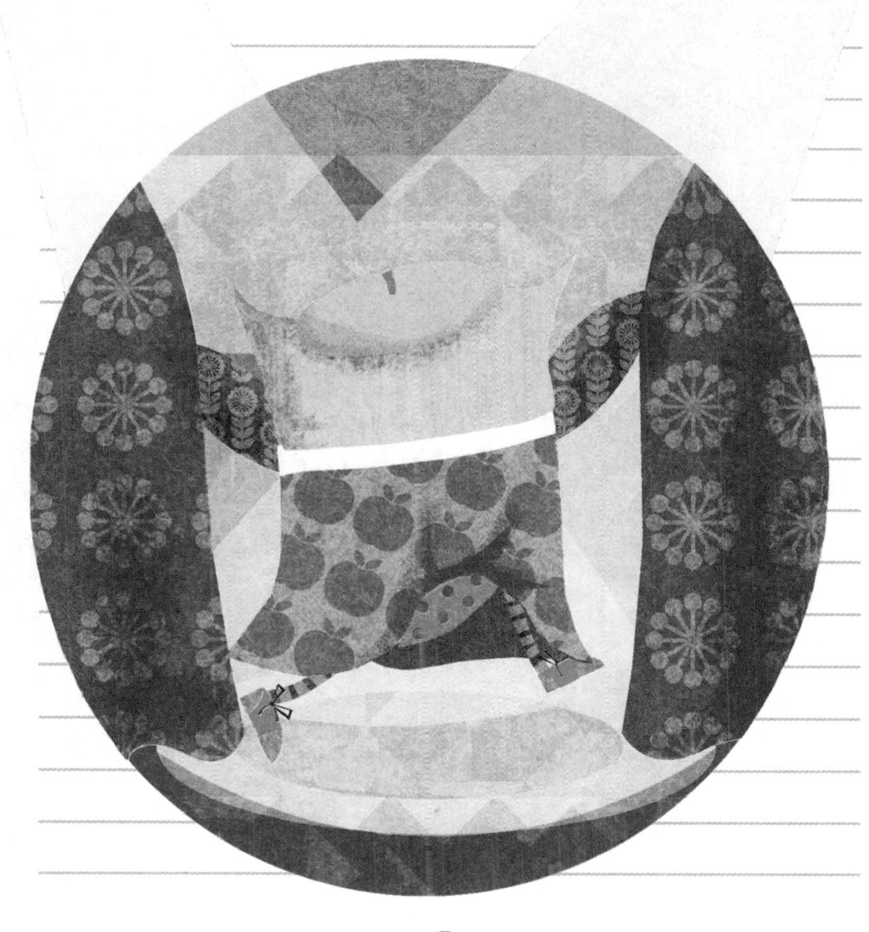

ARGH! The whole festival was so **FEATHER-FLAPPINGLY** embarrassing! I'm sure everyone thinks I'm a total squirrel-head.

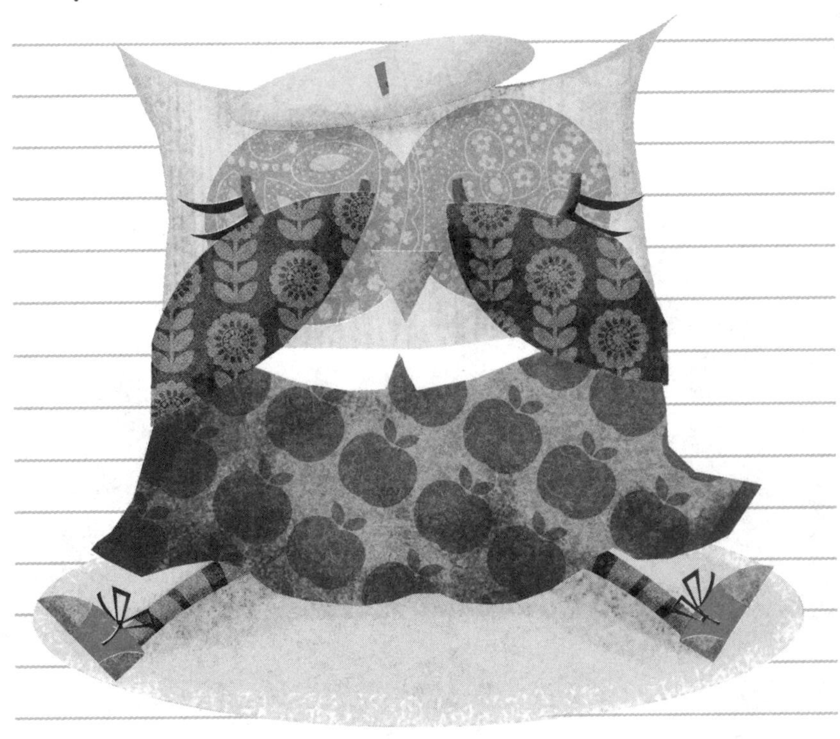

After Miss Featherbottom gives out the contest prizes tomorrow, I hope that I never have to hear about this festival again!

♡ Blooming Fabulous! ♡

Friday

I went to class early to drop off the contest prizes.

Prizes

Then I tried to hide from everyone.

Miss Featherbottom started **HOOTING**:

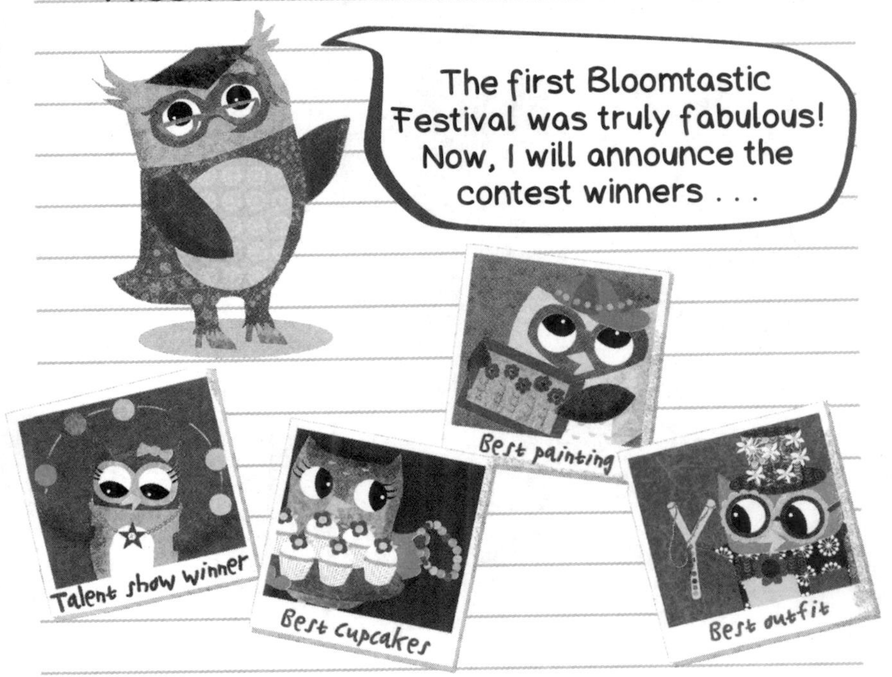
The first Bloomtastic Festival was truly fabulous! Now, I will announce the contest winners . . .
Best painting
Talent show winner
Best cupcakes
Best outfit

Everyone liked the prizes I made. (I felt bad that Lucy didn't win. I never should have helped her with those cupcakes!)

Then, Miss Featherbottom asked me to come up front. I thought she was going to **SCREECH** at me for showing my underpants! But instead . . .

. . . she gave me a special prize!

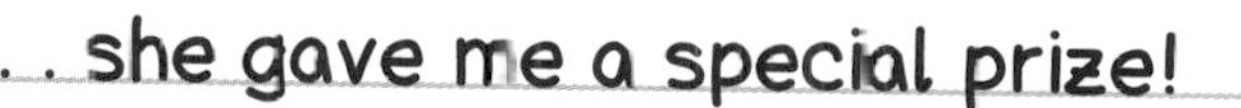

Thank you, Eva, for working so hard and for getting the whole class to work together! We couldn't have had this amazing festival without you.

I was so happy! But I knew that it wouldn't be right to take the prize.

Best Spring Festival Organizer
I'm sorry, but I cannot accept this trophy.
Can all of my classmates come up here, please?

My classmates flew up front. Lucy stood next to me.

This festival never would have happened without the help of all of you.
Best Spring Festival Organizer

We all took turns holding the trophy. Miss Featherbottom smiled. Everyone **HOOTED** and cheered! Even Sue!

Diary, it was the best feeling ever.

Now I just need to think of my next project!

Hmm . . . How soon can I start planning a summer festival?

OWL
DIARIES

How much do you know about Eva's Treetop Festival?

Name some cool owl facts.

Eva creates the word <u>bloomtastic</u>. This word is made up of two real words: <u>bloom</u> and <u>fantastic</u>. What do you think <u>bloomtastic</u> means?

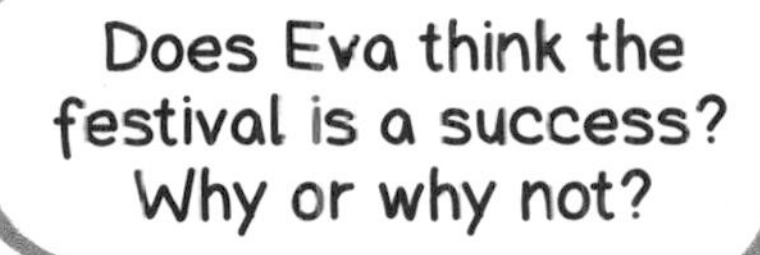
Does Eva think the
festival is a success?
Why or why not?

How does Eva feel about me at the beginning of the story and at the end? What does Eva learn about teamwork?

Would you want to take part in the fashion show, talent show, art show, or bake-off? Use words and pictures to describe what you would do.

scholastic.com/branches

BRANCHES™

OWL DIARIES

Eva Sees a Ghost

Rebecca Elliott

SCHOLASTIC

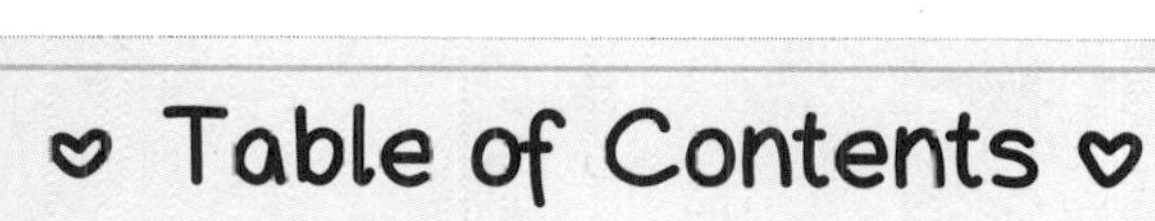

Table of Contents

1 Hello!

Sunday

Hello Diary,

It's me – Eva Wingdale! Did you miss me? I bet you did!

I love:

Drawing

Patterns

Daydreaming

The word plum

Funky hats

QUESTIONNAIRE

1. What is your name?
2. What's your favorite color?
3. What's your favorite food?
4. How tall are you?
5. How fast can you fly?

Questionnaires

My friends

Being super excited!

I DO NOT love:

My brother Humphrey's horrible singing

Sue Clawson ("Meany McMeanerson")

The color gray

Washing my feathers

Being scared

Squirrels

Mom's caterpillar sandwiches

Feeling lonely

Here is my family:

Dad
Mom
Baby Mo
Humphrey
Me

And here is my pet bat, Baxter!

He's so cuddly!

By the way, I'm an owl!
And owls are awesome.

We can fly.

We sleep in the daytime.

We're awake in the nighttime!

And we live in trees.

9

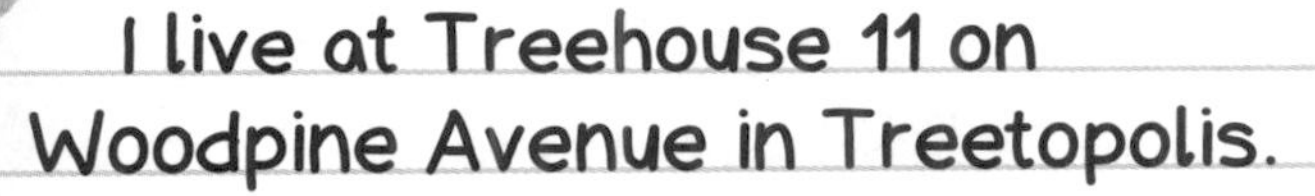

I live at Treehouse 11 on Woodpine Avenue in Treetopolis.

11

My BEST friend is Lucy Beakman. She lives in the tree next door.

We have sleepovers all the time! Our next one is on Sunday – one week from today! Yay!

Lucy has a pet lizard named Rex. Rex is Baxter's best friend, too!

Lucy and I go to Treetop Owlementary. Here is a photo of our class:

Miss Featherbottom
Zac
Macy
Lilly
Carlos
my class
Sue
Jacob
Lucy
Me
George
Zara

I'm off to school now. Talk to you tomorrow, Diary!

No One Believes Me

Monday

Miss Featherbottom read our class a spooky story tonight.

It was a dark and stormy day . . .

Everyone was in a flap after Miss Featherbottom finished reading!

But Lucy and I were TOO excited about our AMAZING SLEEPOVER to be scared by a silly story. (Well, maybe we were just a tiny bit scared.)

At lunch, we planned our sleepover activities.

Things we'll do at Sunday's sleepover:
- Bake worm muffins
- Braid beads into our feathers
- Draw pictures of kittens wearing hats
- Give our pets makeovers
- Stay up for a daytime snack

The sleepover was all I could think about on the flight home. I was flying with Lucy, Carlos, Sue, and Zac when it happened! I SAW A GHOST! There was a white, shimmery blur floating right above us!

Look! A ghost!

But by the time they looked up, the ghost was gone.

Everyone laughed.

Good joke, Eva!

No, really!
I really did just see a ghost!

Ha-ha!
Very funny!

Then Sue said something not so nice.

Oh, stop flapping, Eva. You just made that up. Everyone knows ghosts aren't real!

So now you can see why I call Sue "Meany McMeanerson"! She is SO mean!

This ghost WAS real. I didn't make it up! (This is not like the time I didn't do my math homework because I said I was allergic to the number two. I totally made that up.)

I was upset that no one believed me.

Then Lucy whispered in my ear.

I believe you, Eva.

She really is the best friend in the whole **OWLIVERSE**.

When I got home, I told Humphrey about the ghost. He laughed.

Did the ghost go boo or ooo? If it didn't say boo or ooo, then it wasn't a real ghost.

He's such a squirrel-head. Maybe he's right, though. The ghost didn't go boo. Or ooo.

I guess Miss Featherbottom's spooky story could have made my imagination go a bit crazy.

But I really did see something, Diary! So I need to prove to everyone that there is a ghost in Treetopolis. My mission:

Find the ghost!

It Chased Me!

Tuesday

Hi Diary,

I saw the ghost again tonight!! This time, I was by myself near the Old Oak Tree when I heard a twig snap.

SNAP!

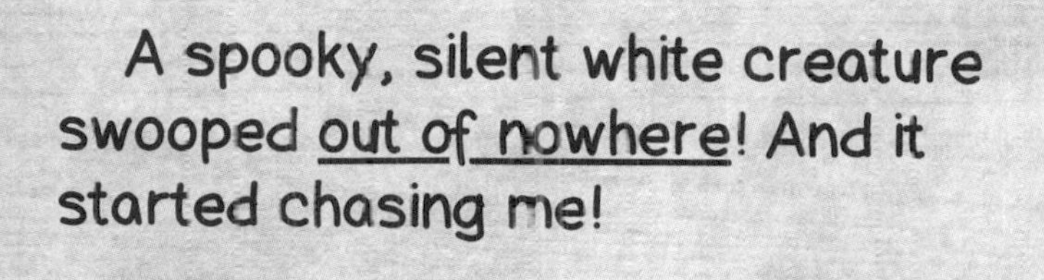

A spooky, silent white creature swooped out of nowhere! And it started chasing me!

I flew through the trees. It was right on my tail feathers!

All of a sudden, there was a huge clap of thunder and lightning!

I flew down to the ground — then up, up almost to the stars. And still it chased me!

I think the ghost wanted to eat me. (I did eat lots of yummy berries and bugs tonight. So I guess I would taste pretty good.)

I dived into a swamp to hide.
I waited there for a bit.

Then I flew home as fast as my
swampy wings could carry me.

Now I KNOW I'm not making anything up! This ghost is NOT in my imagination. It is REAL.

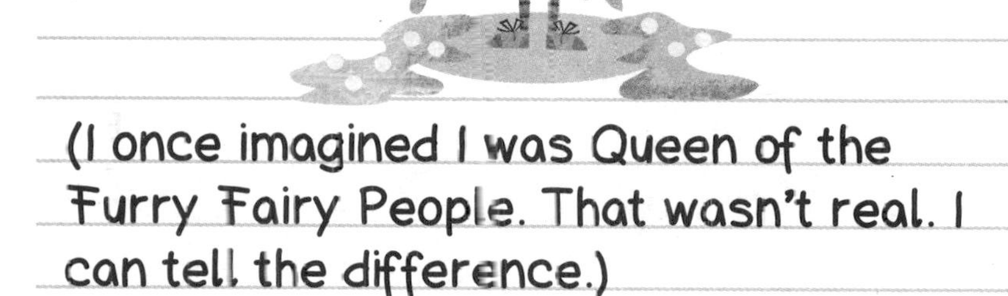

(I once imagined I was Queen of the Furry Fairy People. That wasn't real. I can tell the difference.)

I've put Baxter
on guard-bat duty.

I'm going to take a bath. Then I'm
going to go talk to my friends and
neighbors. I'll ask if they have seen
anything strange in the forest. I can't be
the only one who has seen the ghost.

I love questionnaires. So I'm going
to give each owl a list of questions to
answer.

Here is what I've come up with:

QUESTIONNAIRE

1. What is your name? ____________

2. How smart are you?
☐genius ☐smart ☐average ☐squirrel

3. Where do you live?
☐forest floor ☐swamp ☐tree trunk
☐nest ☐barn

4. Have you SEEN anything strange or scary in the forest (apart from my brother Humphrey)? ____________

5. Have you HEARD anything strange or scary in the forest (apart from Humphrey's windy bottom)? ____________
____
____
____

6. Do you believe in ghosts?
☐yes ☐no ☐maybe

I'll let you know how things go, Diary. It has been a long night and I'm off to bed. Good day.

4 Proof

Wednesday

Hi Diary,

I gave questionnaires to every owl I could find – thirty-five in all! Then Lucy and I collected them back.

Most of the forms look something like Humphrey's:

QUESTIONNAIRE

1. What is your name? Humphrey

2. How smart are you?
☒genius ☐smart ☐average ☐squirrel
I think I'm a genius. You think I'm a squirrel.

3. Where do you live?
☐forest floor ☐swamp ☒tree trunk
☐nest ☐barn Tree trunk – in a bedroom next to yours. Remember?

4. Have you SEEN anything strange or scary in the forest (apart from my brother Humphrey)? Hey! But no.

5. Have you HEARD anything strange or scary in the forest (apart from Humphrey's windy bottom)? Hey again! But no. I haven't heard anything strange. The forest is very noisy though, with all the work-owls building those new fancy tree houses.

6. Do you believe in ghosts?
☐yes ☒no ☐maybe
But I do believe that ninja robot-monkeys will one day rule the world.

Okay, so most owls did not see or hear anything strange. But three owls DID!

Nanny Beakin said she heard whooshing sounds coming from very high up — above the trees! (That's higher than most of us fly. IT MUST BE THE GHOST!)

Mr. Twitteroo said he found this white feather outside his house. I think the ghost has EATEN someone and this is all that is left! (It cannot be anyone I know because I don't know anyone with white feathers.)

Jacob said he heard a boo sound. Then he said it may have been a cow saying moo. I like Jacob. He is a bit of a squirrel-head, though.

This information is helpful. But it is still not enough to prove that the ghost is real.

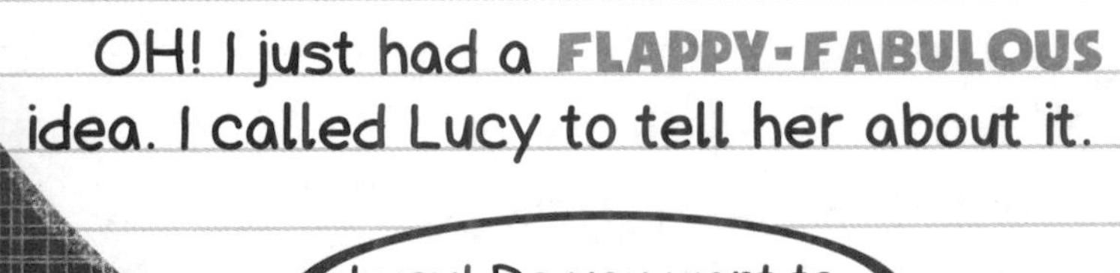

OH! I just had a **FLAPPY-FABULOUS** idea. I called Lucy to tell her about it.

Lucy! Do you want to go on a ghost hunt tomorrow?

That sounds a bit scary, Eva. But let's do it!

Great! We'll fly to the Old Oak Tree after school. That's where I saw it the other day.

Yes! And I'll bring my camera to get a photo of the ghost. Then everyone can see it!

We'll bring some snacks, too, right?

Of course!

I have to get some rest now. I'll need lots and lots of energy for our BIG GHOST HUNT tomorrow!

5

Boo!

Thursday

Oh, Diary!

Tonight was NOT a good night at school.

I was nightdreaming about being a famous ghost hunter.

Then Miss Featherbottom came into class. She has a very LOUD voice.

When she **HOOTED**, I fell off my chair!

Hello, class!

It was so embarrassing. Everyone laughed. Sue called me a scaredy-owl.

Then, at lunchtime, I was eating my **SLUGERONI AND CHEESE** when Humphrey snuck up behind me.

BOO!

I threw my lunch into the air.

Everyone laughed again. Then they ALL started talking about how I think I saw a ghost.

They all think I'm a squirrel-head. I HAVE to prove to them that I didn't make up the ghost.

I'm so glad this stinky school night is over. Now Lucy and I are going to go on our ghost hunt. We just put on cool ghost-hunter outfits. Look!

Now we're ready. I'll let you know how it goes. Wish us luck, Diary!

The Ghost Hunt

Friday

Lucy and I flew to the Old Oak Tree after school yesterday. We sat there and waited.

And waited.

And ate our snacks.

And waited some more.

At one point, Grandpa Owlfred flew past. He's building the fancy new owl tree houses.

Hello, dears! Lovely night!
Shhhh!
We're ghost-hunting!
That's wonderful. Byeee!

We chatted about our sleepover while we waited.

I can't wait for our sleepover on Sunday!
It's going to be flap-tastic!!

We waited some more. Then Lucy said something surprising.

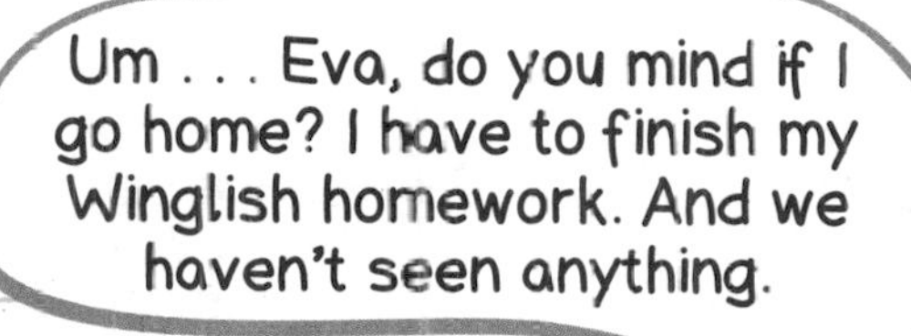
Um . . . Eva, do you mind if I go home? I have to finish my Winglish homework. And we haven't seen anything.
You don't believe me anymore. Do you?
Of course I do!
Really?
Well, I believe you think you saw something.
I don't think I saw something. I really DID see something.
I know. Please don't get your feathers in a flap! I really do have homework to do. Look, you should keep the camera for if—I mean when—you see something. I'll see you tomorrow. Okay?

How could Lucy leave me?! Now NO ONE believes me. Not even my best friend! I hope you still believe me, Diary!

After Lucy left, I waited some more. I sat by the Old Oak Tree until it was almost daylight. I felt sleepy.

THEN . . .

WHOOSH!

The white ghostly figure swooped right past me! It made a booming boo sound!! (Well, it may have been a loud hoot sound or even a moo sound. It was hard to tell. But I definitely heard an oooo noise!)

I was SO scared, Diary! And my wings were shaking SO much that I could hardly hold Lucy's camera.

CLICK!

The photo came out blurry. But at least I finally have PROOF that the ghost is real!

I've never been as scared as I was last night, Diary. I don't know how I got <u>any</u> sleep!

I'm going to take this photo to school tonight. I'll show everyone that I <u>am</u> telling the truth!

7 Spooky School!

Saturday

I carried my ghost photo into school last night.

Treetop Owlementary

Soon, it was time for show-and-tell.

Who would like to share first?

I flew to the front of the class.

I have something to show!
What is that?
It's a photo of the ghost! I saw it again!
It doesn't look like a ghost.
It's a ghost!
Listen, if Eva says that's a picture of a ghost, then that's what it is. She doesn't make things up!
Thanks, Lucy!

I showed the photo again. But the other owlets just laughed.

I flew back to my seat.

Miss Featherbottom asked everyone to quiet down. Then she put her wing around me.

Your photo is blurry, Eva. That makes it hard to see what this is a picture of. I love that you have such an amazing imagination though! That gives me an idea!

Let's all tell our best scary stories. And whoever tells the scariest story gets to ring Barry the Bell!

Everyone loves ringing Barry the Bell. So everyone wanted to tell a scary story.

George told a story about zombie squirrels.

Macy told one about giant spiders.

And Lilly was halfway through telling a story about fire-breathing dragons when . . .

BAM!

There was a LOUD noise on the roof!

We all went quiet. Our beaks were wide open. Our wings were shaking. Even our teacher looked scared.

BAM!

There it was again! Something BIG was up on the roof!

No more spooky stories. Stay here, owlets. I'll find out what's making that noise.

I rushed to the window and opened it. I stuck my beak out to try to look up at the roof. Everyone crowded around.

Eva, cl-cl-close the window!
I know what I'm doing!
Look!

We saw two ghostly white beasts swooping high above us.

Eva, you were t-t-telling the truth!
There are TWO ghosts?!
It's all a blur! They are moving so fast!

Everyone started saying they were sorry. Then Lucy tugged on my wing.

Eva, I'm sorry I didn't believe you the whole time.
That's okay. I probably wouldn't have believed me, either!

I'm so happy Lucy believes me again!

Miss Featherbottom came back. She said there was nothing to worry about.

We all looked at one another, but nobody said anything. Would she believe us if we told her we saw ghosts?

We were all quiet. Then Sue raised her wing.

Um, Miss Featherbottom, we think Eva should get to ring the bell. Her ghost story was the scariest!

I couldn't believe it! Sue said _I_ should ring the bell! I smiled at her. And I rang that bell as loudly as I could!

Bing-a-ling-a-ling!

At lunch, we came up with a plan.

Let's all go on a Treetop Owlementary Ghost Hunt tomorrow!
Yes! Together, we'll catch the ghosts!
We'll need some ghost-catching tools!
Let's make a ghost-hunting kit after school!

So, Diary, the good news is: Everyone believes me now. But the bad news is: Treetopolis is haunted!

Uh-oh! I have to go! It's almost time for the ghost hunt!

♡ The Ghost Group ♡

Sunday

Yesterday, we all went on the Treetop Owlementary Ghost Hunt. We took our ghost-hunting kit to the Old Oak Tree.

Macy and Zac brought a huge ghost-catching net.

George and Lilly brought a big water-balloon-throwing slingshot.

Zara and Carlos brought binoculars for looking far away.

Jacob and Sue brought a blanket for us all to hide under.

And Lucy and I brought Ghost Hunter costumes for everyone.

We were ready!

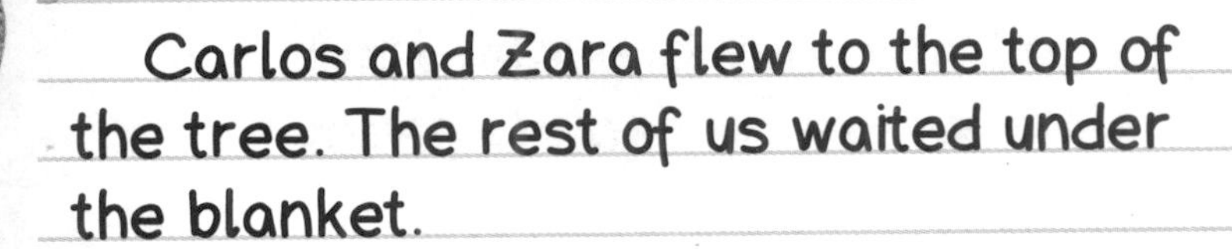

Carlos and Zara flew to the top of the tree. The rest of us waited under the blanket.

Suddenly, Zara saw something.

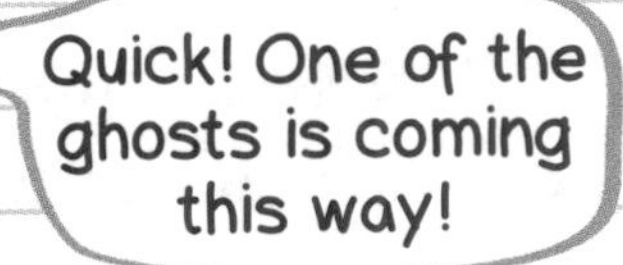
Quick! One of the ghosts is coming this way!

George loaded the slingshot. Lilly pulled it back.

ATTACK!

The huge white ghost whooshed past us. SPLAT! Lilly and George missed.

The beast flew toward us again.

WHOOSH!

Macy and Zac threw the net. It landed right on top of the ghost!

We got it!!

Everyone else was still hiding under the blanket. So I was the only one who finally got a good look at the ghost. But it was too late.

Diary, it was so **HOOTINGLY** horrible!

I flew toward the net.

What's Eva doing?
I don't know, but I'm not going near the ghost!
Quick! Everyone! Come help me!

The other owlets were too scared to come out from under the blanket. They're such scaredy-owls.

But Lucy flew over. She helped me untangle the net.

The ghost wasn't a ghost at all . . .

It was an owl!

What did you do that for?

I'm so sorry!

We thought you were a ghost.

A ghost? I'm not a ghost! I'm a snowy owl!

Then four more white owls swooped down from the trees. They landed next to Lucy and me.

Dad, they thought we were ghosts!

The big, white snowy owl started to laugh. He laughed so hard he was holding his belly.

Our family is moving to Treetopolis. We've been flying around to check on our new tree house and to get to know our new town.
But why did one of you chase me the other day?
That was me. I was trying to warn you that a storm was coming!
Oh. Thank you.

And why did you bang on the school roof?
That was me. I can't fly very well yet. I flew into the roof! Then Dad came down to get me.
Oh.

Our classmates had questions for the snowy owls, too.

And were you flying really high?
Yes. I got lost. So I was flying up high to look for my new tree house.

And were you making loud hooting noises?
Yep, that was us, too. In our old town, everyone had a deep hoot. That's just how we speak.

By the way, I'm Eva. This is my best friend, Lucy.
It's lovely to meet you. I'm Kiera.
Hi!

Our classmates all met Kiera.

Hello.
Glad you're not a ghost.

Then Kiera's family and the other owlets flew off.

This was the best ghost hunt ever!

We're sorry about what happened.
And I'm really sorry I thought you were a ghost.

Just then, I had the best idea ever! I whispered it to Lucy.

Lucy stepped forward.

Kiera, Eva and I are having a sleepover tomorrow. Would you like to come, too?

I'd love to!

Now I need to go get ready for our big sleepover. Lucy, Kiera, and I are going to have the best sleepover ever!

So, Diary, I thought I'd found a ghost. But, really, I'd found something much better: a new friend.

OWL DIARIES

How much do you know about Eva Sees a Ghost?

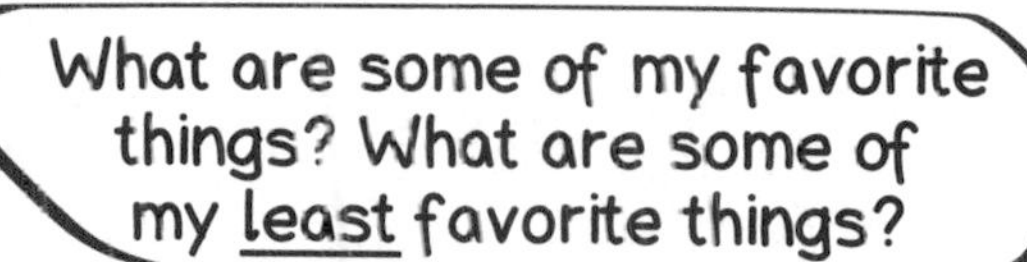

What are some of my favorite things? What are some of my least favorite things?

How does Eva feel when her classmates don't believe her? What happens that changes the way her classmates think about the ghost?

What not-so-nice things do I do throughout this story? How do I surprise Eva?

Use examples from the book to describe the ghost that Eva sees. Then write or draw pictures to show the truth!

Create a questionnaire to learn more about your friends! Share it with them. Then talk about your discoveries!

OWL DIARIES

BRANCHES™

A Woodland Wedding

Rebecca Elliott

SCHOLASTIC

♡ Table of Contents ♡

11
Woodpine Avenue
9

Hello There!

Sunday

Hello Diary,

I'm back! It's ME – Eva Wingdale! I wonder what fun we're going to have together this week!

I love:

Painting

TO DO:
1.
2.
3.
4.
5.

Writing to-do lists

The smell of strawberries

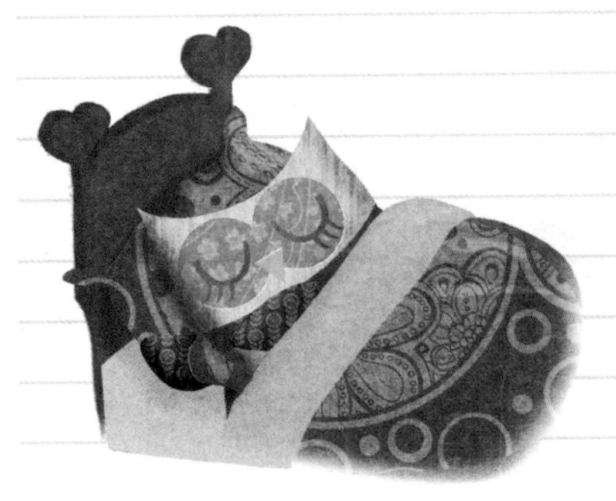

My pillow

Reading mysteries

The word lollipop

Bluebells
(my favorite flower)

Laughing with
my friends

I DO NOT love:

My brother Humphrey's LOUD guitar playing (He's good, but he's so NOISY!)

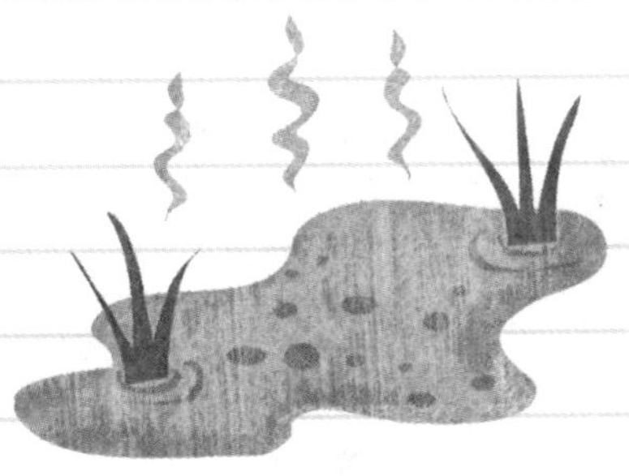

The word swamp

Sue Clawson (when she's mean)

MEANY
McMEANERSON
100555

Brushing my feathers

Rainy nights

The smell of
squirrel poop

Mom's worm cake

Seeing anyone
feeling sad

I totally LOVE my family!

Here we are on vacation in sunny **OWLIFORNIA**:

HOWLYWOOD
Dad
Humphrey
Me
Baby Mo
Mom

My pet bat, Baxter, is part of my family, too.

He's so sweet!

And I LOVE being an owl!

Owls do all sorts of cool things — like fly SUPER fast.

We stay awake ALL night.

We sleep in the daytime.

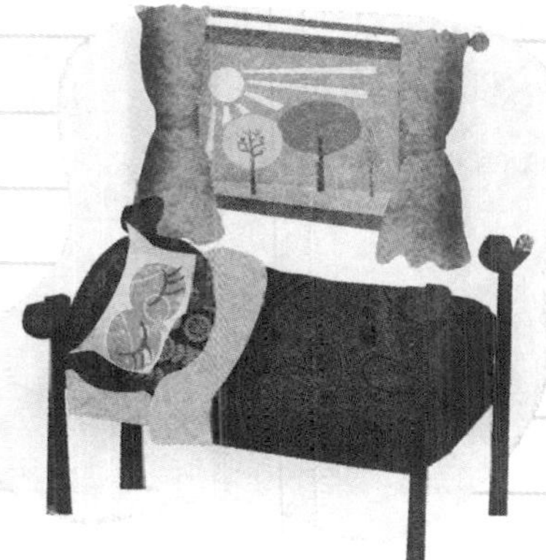

And we see things really far away with our BIG eyes.

I live at Treehouse 11 on Woodpine Avenue in Treetopolis.

My best friend is Lucy Beakman.

11
9

Lucy lives next door! We talk on our **PINEPHONES** all the time.

Lucy has a pet lizard named Rex. Rex is Baxter's best friend. We love dressing up our pets!

Lucy and I go to school together. Here is a photo of our class:

Miss Featherbottom
Sue
Kiera
Zara
Macy
my class
Zac
George
Me
Lucy
Jacob
Lilly
Carlos

It's almost sunrise. I need to go to sleep. Talk to you tomorrow, Diary!

2

A Mystery Owl

Monday

Miss Featherbottom told us some very exciting news tonight.

Tomorrow is Pet Day. That means you can bring your pets to school with you!

How **FLAPERRIFIC** is that, Diary?! I can't wait for everyone to meet Baxter!

We drew pictures of our pets.

Rex
Gumdrop
General Slithers

Kiera drew the best picture. So she got to ring Barry the Bell. We all love ringing Barry the Bell.

Bing-a-ling-a-ling!

We were getting ready to fly home when we saw a handsome **OWLMAN** waiting outside for Miss Featherbottom. They started smiling at each other, and then they stood wing-in-wing!

Treetop Owlementary

We wondered who the owl might be . . .

Perhaps he's her brother?
Or her cousin?
Or her wing doctor?
Maybe he's giving her dance lessons?
Or maybe he's her boyfriend!

Everyone giggled.

Lucy came over to my tree house after school. We talked about Miss Featherbottom's mystery friend.

I hope he IS her boyfriend.
They looked so happy together!
They really did! But now we need to stop chatting and get on with planning tomorrow's Pet Day!
Should we dress up our pets?
Yes! And why don't we decorate Rex's and Baxter's cages, too?
That's a flap-tastic idea, Eva!

We dressed up our pets as kings. And we turned their cages into castles – to match their king costumes. We even decorated their castles with sparkly jewels!

I can't wait to meet everyone's pets! Sleep tight, Diary!

3

Pet Day

Tuesday

Today was **FLAPPY-FABULOUS**, Diary! The pets were ALL cute!

Flash: Jacob's giant snail

General Slithers: George's snake

Sid: Zac's spider

Steve: Lilly's moth

Clive:
Carlos's goldfish

Rex:
Lucy's lizard

Baxter:
Eva's bat

Susan Wilkinson:
Zara's crab

Wilber:
Macy's tree frog

Gumdrop:
Kiera's bumblebee

Lady:
Sue's tortoise

And guess what! Because Rex's and Baxter's costumes looked SO great, Lucy and I got to ring Barry the Bell!

Bing-a-ling-a-ling!

At lunch, our class had a Pet Picnic. We ate **BUG BURGERS** and **FLY FRIES** and we gave our pets critter treats, blueberry chews, and saucers of milk!

Then Miss Featherbottom had big news to share . . .

The friend you saw me with last night is Mr. Plumage. He is my boyfriend. And we are getting married THIS SATURDAY!

You're ALL invited to the wedding! And because your pets have been so good today, they're invited, too!

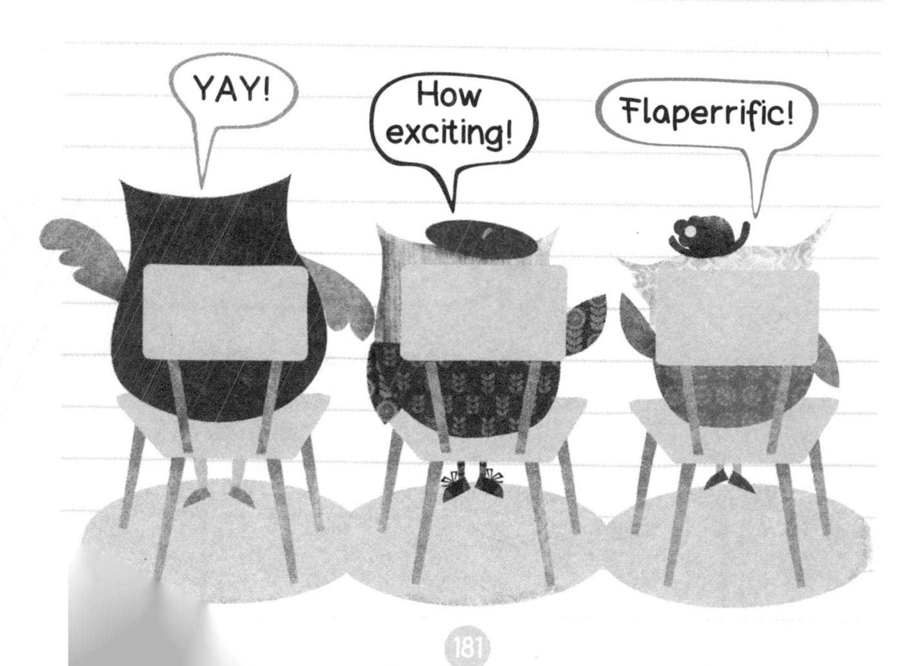
YAY!
How exciting!
Flaperrific!

Please quiet down. I need your help, owlets. A tradition is something that's always done. And one wedding tradition is that the bride – that's me – has to wear something old, something new, something borrowed, and something blue. I already have my something old . . .

Miss Featherbottom took a beautiful necklace out of her desk drawer. It was super shiny, with beautiful jewels!

This belonged to my grandmother. It's very old!

Now I need you to help me come up with the rest of the items. What could I wear for something new, borrowed, and blue?

We called out ideas.
You could get a NEW feathercut?
You could BORROW my shoes? But they might not fit.
You could paint your feathers BLUE?
Flap-tastic suggestions! Thank you! Okay, time for your Winglish lesson.

I went to Lucy's house after school. We made wedding dresses from old sheets. And we dressed Rex and Baxter as grooms!

9

But then Sue Clawson flew by and said something REALLY mean.

You two look more like crazy ghosts than brides! Why are you playing weddings anyway? Weddings are SOOO squirrelly!

This is why sometimes I call Sue "Meany McMeanerson." How could anyone think weddings are squirrelly? Sue might not like weddings, but I LOVE them!

Now I'm off to bed to dream of my perfect wedding dress. Sweet dreams, Diary!

The Secret Wedding Club

Wednesday

I got to school super early today. I did not want to miss anything Miss Featherbottom said about the wedding! But when I got to class she looked sad.

What's wrong?
Nothing really. I'm just worried because Saturday is soon and there's a lot to do for the wedding!

I felt sorry for Miss Featherbottom. I really wanted to help her.

At recess we all played weddings. Well, all of us except for Sue. She wanted to play jump rope games and got mad when no one wanted to play.

My game is much more fun than your stinky wedding game!

Then Meany McMeanerson flew off in a flap.

All during recess I kept worrying about Miss Featherbottom. Then I had a great idea! I called everyone over . . .

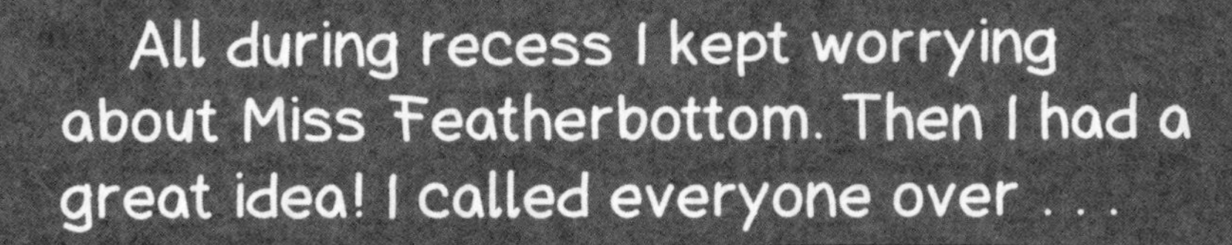
I'm going to start an after-school Secret Wedding Planners Club! We'll plan wedding things to help Miss Featherbottom. Who wants to join?
Sounds fun!
Great idea, Eva!
I'm in!
I'll join!
Me, too!
No, thank you. I have more important things to do.

After school our club had our first meeting. We wrote a wedding to-do list.

1. Bake a cake
2. Make decorations (garlands, balloons, tablecloths)
3. Pick flowers for the bouquets
4. Find a band

Next, we all flew to my house, picking flowers as we went. (I always pick bluebells!)

Then we made an **OWLSOME** cake!

And we had a flour fight!

I need to wash my feathers and get to sleep. There's still so much to do. But we should be fine — so long as nothing goes wrong tomorrow. And I'm sure nothing will go wrong. Right?!

The Missing Necklace

Thursday

Disaster! When we got to school Miss Featherbottom looked really sad.

Class, I have bad news. My special necklace – the something old that I was going to wear at my wedding – is missing!

The Secret Wedding Planners Club held an emergency meeting at my tree house after school.

Miss Featherbottom seems so sad!
What can we do?
The best way for us to help her is to add another task to our to-do list: solve the case of the missing necklace!

We became the Secret Wedding Planners and Detectives Club! I've read LOTS of mystery books. So I knew we needed to do three things: dress like detectives, ask questions, and look for clues. We put on our detective outfits.

Then we flew back to school. Luckily, Miss Featherbottom was still there. Kiera started asking questions.

When did you last see your necklace?
I'm not sure exactly. I remember having it in my desk on Tuesday because it was Pet Day. And I remember General Slithers crawling through it. But I can't remember if I saw it after that.
Has anything else gone missing?
Well, now that I think about it, I couldn't find my silver star stickers or glitter pens this morning.

Next, we searched for clues. Zara pointed to Miss Featherbottom's desk.

Miss Featherbottom
Look at these scratch marks! Isn't this the drawer where the necklace was kept?
Yes. But the necklace isn't in the classroom anymore. And neither is the thief. Let's go search the forest.

No one paid much attention to the scratch marks. But I felt like I had seen them before. I just had to remember where!

We searched the forest for ages. Finally, George saw something.

Who's that over there?
It's Sue.
Look! Her bag has something shiny sticking out of it!
And Sue doesn't like weddings!
Maybe she took the necklace!

We flew over to Sue.

What's in your bag, Sue?
None of your business.
Did you pick up Miss Featherbottom's necklace – maybe by mistake? Do you maybe have it in your bag?
I am not a thief, Eva! I didn't take the necklace!

Sue looked upset as she flew away. I felt awful. Oh, Diary! I guess I said the wrong thing? I was only trying to solve the mystery!

The club flew back to my house. We couldn't solve the mystery tonight, but we could work on other items from the to-do list.

Carlos and George blew up balloons.

Kiera and Zara picked flowers.

Lucy and I made garlands.

My brother Humphrey told us we were squirrel-heads for getting so excited about a wedding.

But we all got a lot done! And we had a **HOOT**! We couldn't wait to show Miss Featherbottom tomorrow!

After the other owlets left, I asked Lucy about Sue . . .

I don't really think Sue took the necklace. Do you?
No, I don't think so. But why doesn't she like weddings?
I don't know, Lucy. But I feel bad for asking her if she took the necklace. She looked really upset.
Why don't we fly past her house in the morning to say sorry?
Great idea, Lucy!

Lucy really is the best friend in the whole **OWLIVERSE**. I promise to apologize to Sue AND solve the case tomorrow!

6

Meany Mystery Solved!

Friday

Lucy and I flew over to Sue's house before school. I picked more flowers on the way – you can never have too many bluebells!

But, Diary, you'll never guess what we saw through Sue's window!

Look at that beautiful wedding dress!

We knocked on the door. When Sue answered, she was covered in white silk. It looked like <u>she</u> was wearing a wedding dress!

You didn't want to play wedding with us. But you're playing it on your own?
You said weddings were squirrelly.
Oh. Hi. Just come in. I'll explain everything.

Sue showed us the wedding dress.

Well, my mom is a fashion designer. She's making Miss Featherbottom's dress, and I've been helping her. When you saw me in the forest I was carrying my mom's sequins and sparkly thread.

Oh. Um. That's why we're here . . . I wanted to say I'm sorry for thinking you took the necklace.
That's okay.

Yeah. We thought maybe you took it because we saw something shiny in your bag. And because, well, you seem to not like weddings.
I LOVE weddings! I'm even making Miss Featherbottom a special present. It's just that I've been feeling really mad all week. You see, my mom's been so busy making this dress that I think she's forgotten . . .
Forgotten what?

Sue started to cry.

I think she's forgotten that my birthday is on Sunday.
Oh no! That's awful!
I'm sure she hasn't forgotten, Sue. Is there anything we can do to cheer you up?

I'm not sure. But, well, maybe I could join your club?
Yes, please!
We could use all the help we can get!

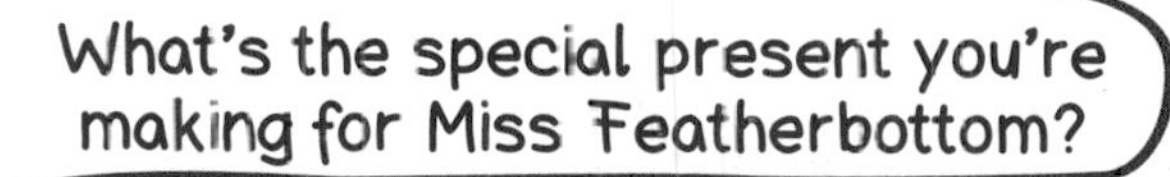
What's the special present you're making for Miss Featherbottom?

A flower crown. But it's only half done. I won't have time to finish it.
I have some bluebells. Can I help?

Sue and I made the flower crown while Lucy helped Sue's mom with the dress. The flower crown really looked **WING-CREDIBLE** – and so did the dress!

Miss Featherbottom smiled when we got to class.

This is a flaperrific surprise! I cannot believe your club made my cake, tablecloths, flowers, and garlands!

(We didn't show her the flower crown or the balloons. We had to keep some surprises for the wedding day!)

This is all so wonderful! But I still need to find a band and my missing necklace.

Poor Miss Featherbottom.

At lunch, we had an emergency club meeting.

We must find a band and solve the mystery of the missing necklace!
But the wedding is TOMORROW!
We'll need to work fast!
Does anyone know where we can find a band?

Just then, my brother Humphrey walked over.

Hey, Eva, do you need a band? My band, The Hootles, could play if you want.

Wow, Humph – that'd be amazing! Nothing too noisy though!
Of course not.

Then he winked, which worried me. But still – YAY! We found a band!

We flew to tell Miss Featherbottom the good news.

We found a wedding band!
Oh, how wonderful!

Then our newest detective took a look around the room. She opened Miss Featherbottom's desk drawer—the one below the scratch marks.

Hey! I may have found another clue!

Sue used her magnifying glass to take a closer look.

Critter-treat crumbs!
From the Pet Picnic! Good work, Sue!
We WILL get to the bottom of this!

After school, our club made another list. (I love making lists.)

THE CASE OF THE MISSING NECKLACE

What we know:

1. The necklace is shiny and sparkly.
2. The necklace was last seen on Tuesday.
3. General Slithers crawled through it.
4. Miss Featherbottom's silver star stickers and glitter pens are also missing.
5. There are scratch marks above Miss Featherbottom's desk drawer.
6. The necklace is not in the classroom or the forest (or Sue's bag).
7. There are crumbs inside the drawer.

What we need to know:

1. Where is the necklace?
2. Who took it?

Diary, the wedding is tomorrow! We must solve the mystery! I'm going to think about the clues as I fall asleep . . .

7

A Woodland Wedding

Saturday

Diary, today is THE day!! Do you like my dress?

Oh, and I THINK I KNOW WHO TOOK THE NECKLACE! But I won't say anything yet. We both know I've been wrong before, and that didn't go well. I need to make sure I'm right before I even tell you my idea.

First, I need to phone Lucy.

Hi, Lucy! The wedding is TODAY!
Yippeeeee!
Hey, I'm bringing Baxter in his castle-cage. Are you bringing Rex in his?
Yes. Should we dress them up, too?
Of course! They can be kings again!
Great idea! But Eva, I feel bad we didn't find the necklace.
Guess what! I think I solved the mystery!
Really? Wow! Tell me more, Eva!
I can't right now. But you'll know everything soon!

Lucy and I flew to the wedding super early to set up. The other club members met us there.

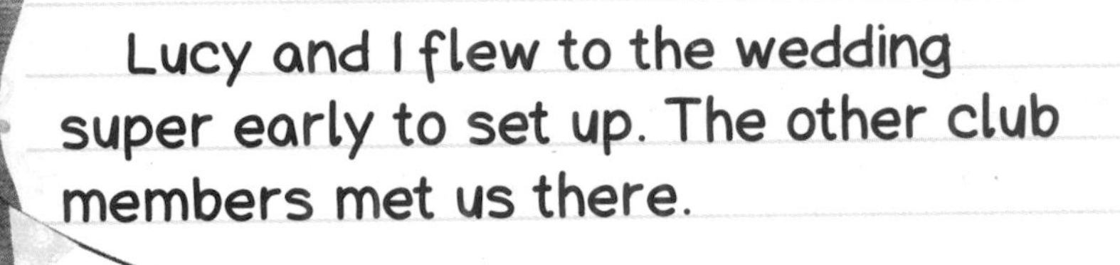
Everything looks flap-tastic!
But we still haven't found the necklace.
Don't worry! Eva thinks she's solved the mystery!
Yes! I think—

Just then, Miss Featherbottom flew in.
Everything looks so beautiful! Thank you all so much! I just wish I had my necklace.
Miss Featherbottom, have you seen Rex and Baxter?
The pets all look lovely, Eva.
But come look at Rex with his castle-cage.
I'm rather busy, Eva.
Please, Miss Featherbottom!
Well, okay.
Look closely, everyone!

We all looked at Rex and at his castle.

My necklace!
Rex took it?! Oh, I'm so sorry!
It's not your fault, dear.
The important thing is that
we found it in time!

Wow, Eva! How did you solve the mystery?
Teamwork! The crumbs Sue found made me sure the thief was a pet. The scratch marks Zara found made me think of Rex. Whenever Rex plays with Baxter he leaves scratch marks all over the tree.
I also know Rex likes shiny things! So I thought he must have taken the necklace, stickers, and glitter pens – all to decorate his castle!
Thank you so much, everyone!

Oh no! I was so worried about my necklace that I forgot my something new, borrowed, or blue! I don't have ANY of those things!

Sue and I looked at each other. We both had the same idea!

We can help you with that!

We handed Miss Featherbottom the flower crown we had made.

It's new, it's blue, and – if you give it back – it's borrowed, too!

Wow! Thank you so much! And it makes me hootingly happy to see you two working together.

Miss Featherbottom flew off to change into her wedding dress.

My dear Diary, the wedding was the most beautiful wedding I have ever seen! (Well, it was also the ONLY wedding I have ever seen! But I can't imagine a lovelier one!)

Later, we all danced to Humphrey's band.

THE HOOTLES

Sue's mom came over and gave me an invitation to a surprise birthday party tomorrow — for Sue! She didn't forget!

I got an invitation!
Me, too!
Hooray! We're all invited!

We danced the day away, Diary! Now I must get some sleep! I can't wait to see Sue's face when she finds out about the surprise tomorrow!! Good day!

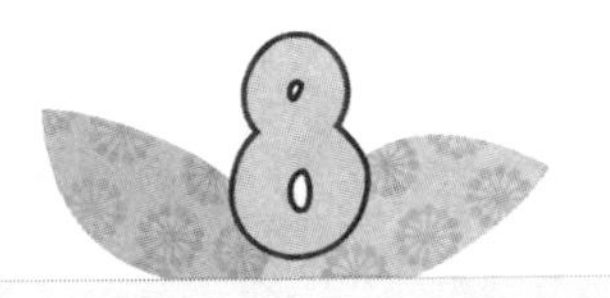

Surprise!

Sunday

Lucy, Kiera, and I flew to Sue's house early to help set up for the party. Other owlets were there, too. (Sue was out having lunch with her dad.)

We reused some balloons from the wedding.

And we painted a birthday banner.

HAPPY BIRTHDAY SUE

Sue's tree house looked beautiful. Soon, we heard Sue flying up. We hid just as the front door opened . . .

Then we all jumped up!

Surprise!
Wow! You didn't forget! Thank you, Mom!
Of course I didn't forget! Happy birthday, darling! And please say thank you to all your friends. They helped set everything up.

Thank you, friends!
You're welcome!
It was fun!
Happy birthday, Sue!

See, Sue? No one could ever forget you!
Thanks, Eva.

A woodland wedding and a surprise party in one weekend! Phew! This has been an amazing week, Diary! I can't wait until next week!

OWL DIARIES

How much do you know about A Woodland Wedding?

Planning a wedding is hard. What do my friends and I do to help Miss Featherbottom?

Miss Featherbottom's necklace is very special. Explain why the necklace is so important to her.

Eva loves reading mystery books – and she learns from them as well! What does Eva learn about how to be a detective? How does Eva use what she learned to solve the mystery of the missing necklace?

Why am I the only owl who is not super excited for the wedding?

Write a diary entry about a party you've attended. Explain the reason for the party, describe the decorations, list the guests, and add any other fun details!

scholastic.com/branches

BRANCHES™

OWL DIARIES

Eva and the New Owl

Rebecca Elliott

SCHOLASTIC

Table of Contents

11
Woodpine Avenue

1 I'm Back!

Thursday

Hello Diary,

Look who's back! It's me — Eva Wingdale! Your feathery friend!

I love:

Writing stories

Stargazing

Picnics

My new slippers

Blueberry ice cream

Playing **WINGBALL**

The word bumblebee

Sleepovers

I DO NOT love:

The word slime

Tying my shoelaces

Spelling tests

Mom's bug salad

Washing dishes

Baby Mo's
stinky diapers

Squirrels stealing
our food (unless it's
Mom's bug salad)

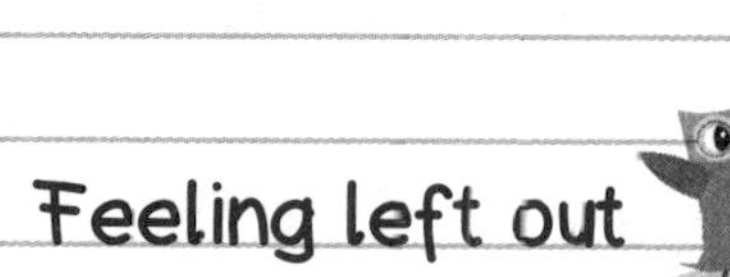

Feeling left out

I REALLY love my family!

Here's our holiday card picture:

Dad
Mom
the Wingdales
Humphrey
Baby Mo
Me

I also love my pet bat, Baxter. He's part of the family, too!

Owls are amazing. I love, love, love being an owl!

We are awake ALL night.

We are asleep ALL day.

We can fly without making any noise.

Shhh!

And we can hear things a long way away.

11
9

I live at Treehouse 11 on Woodpine Avenue in Treetopolis.

My next-door neighbor is my BEST friend, Lucy Beakman.

Lucy has a pet lizard named Rex. Rex and Baxter are best friends. We love dressing up our pets.

Rex

Lucy and I go to school together. Here is our class photo:

Mrs. Featherbottom
Kiera
Zac
Macy
Sue
Carlos
my class
Lilly
Zara
Me
Jacob
George
Lucy

Now I need to get to bed because I have school tomorrow. Bye, Diary!

The Owl Times

Friday

School was so much fun tonight, Diary! Mrs. Featherbottom told us about a new project we'll be working on this week.

We are going to create a class newspaper called the Owl Times! Everyone will have a special job.

We each chose a job . . .

Carlos:
cartoonist

Zac:
weather reporter

Macy:
editor

Lilly:
sports reporter

Sue:
fashion writer

Zara:
photographer

Jacob:
travel writer

George:
designer

Lucy:
crossword puzzle
writer

I chose news reporter. It was the perfect job for me! I love asking questions. And I love writing.

Everyone was excited about their jobs – especially Zara! She started taking photos right away!

CLICK!
CLICK!
CLICK!
CLICK!

The first piece of news I heard was from Mrs. Featherbottom:

There will be a contest this week! Principal Eggmington will choose the best forest drawing!

The winning drawing will be published in our newspaper. And the winner will win two movie tickets to <u>Wingderella</u>!

Wow! I hope I win, Diary! I'd give my extra ticket to Lucy so we could see **WINGDERELLA** together!!

At recess, I talked to my classmates and kept my ears open for more news. Here's what I found out:

George has a new hat.

Kiera and her family are on vacation in **HOOTALULU**.

Hello from Hootalulu

Sue's mom is designing a dress for famous actress Fifi Flyaway.

Macy's pet frog, Wilber, won "Best in Show" last weekend.

1

This news was all exciting. But I heard the <u>best</u> news after recess . . .

A new owl will be joining our class on Monday. Her name is Hailey Fluffington.

This was **FLAP-TASTIC** news! Everyone spent the rest of the day talking about the new owl.

Lucy and I were both excited to meet Hailey.

I can't wait to show her around!
I can't wait to find out her favorite color!

Now I must get to bed. Good day!

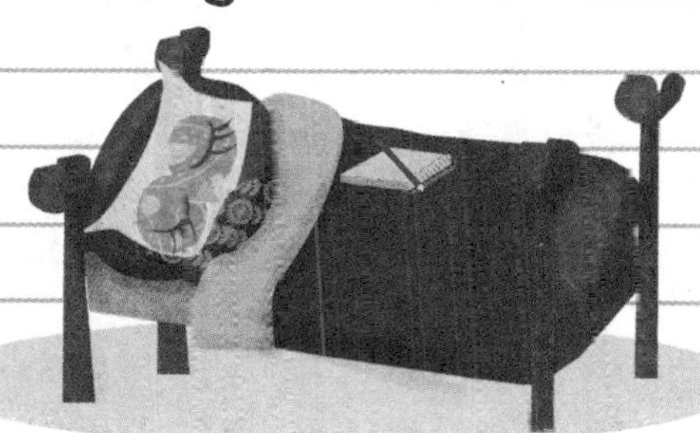

3

♡ Meany McMeanerson! ♡

Saturday

I love being busy, Diary. This is a good thing – because I ended up being crazy busy tonight!

I wrote a to-do list of everything I wanted to get done this weekend. (I even added a couple of things to help make Hailey feel super welcome on her first day at school!)

1. Get my feathers cut
(It is about time!)
2. Draw the best
forest drawing
3. Keep reporting for
the class newspaper
(I'll write down any
news I hear!)
4. Make Hailey a
necklace
5. Make Hailey a guide
to Treetopolis

First, I went to the **FEATHERDRESSER**. But I wasn't the only owl there . . .

Sue Clawson was there! She is always getting her feathers done. And her claws. And her eyelashes. And her wing tips.

Now, Diary, sometimes Sue can be nice. And sometimes Sue can be mean.

Nice Sue
Mean Sue

Sometimes I call her Meany McMeanerson.

MEANY
McMEANERSON
100555

Sadly, today was a Meany day . . .

Oooh, it's about time you got your feathers done, Eva.

Well, I like looking my best, too, Sue.

You know, the new owl is not going to like you just because you've had a few feathers cut.

Who said anything about the new owl?
I heard you and Lucy hooting about her in class. But Hailey's going to choose the coolest owls to be her friends – owls like me!

We'll just see about that, Diary.

Then I flew home to work on my drawing. Lucy stopped by.

Hi, Eva! Do you want to come over?
Sorry, Lucy. I'm coloring my forest drawing.
That looks great! I'll go work on mine now, too! Maybe we can hang out tomorrow?
Maybe! Bye, Lucy!

It took me a LONG time to finish my drawing. But it looks good! I'm just not sure if it's good enough to win. What do you think, Diary?

My to-do list isn't even half finished, but the sun is coming up. It looks like tomorrow is going to be another crazy-busy night! I must get to sleep!

4

♡ Busy, Busy, Busy ♡

Sunday

Tonight started off with some reporting for the newspaper. . .

I heard Mom on the phone with Lilly's mom.

Lilly's mom had just talked to George's mom.

George's little sister Jenny had sprained her wing playing **WINGBALL**.

Poor Jenny!

I called Zara and asked her to meet me at George's house. I interviewed Jenny while Zara took photos.

What did you say when it happened?
Ouch.

When I got home, I still had two things left on my to-do list:

1. Get my feathers cut (it is about time!)
2. Draw the best forest drawing
3. Keep reporting for the class newspaper (I'll write down any news I hear!)
4. Make Hailey a necklace
5. Make Hailey a guide to Treetopolis

I got right to work!

First, I made a **FLAPERRIFIC** bead necklace.

Here it is:

Then Lucy called.
Eva, guess what! I have a new puppet-show theater!
Wow! That's wing-tastic!
Do you want to come over to play with it?
Sorry, but I'm busy making things for Hailey's first day.
That's nice of you! Well, I guess I'll see you at school tomorrow.
Yes! Bye, Lucy!

Finally, I finished the guide. Check it out!

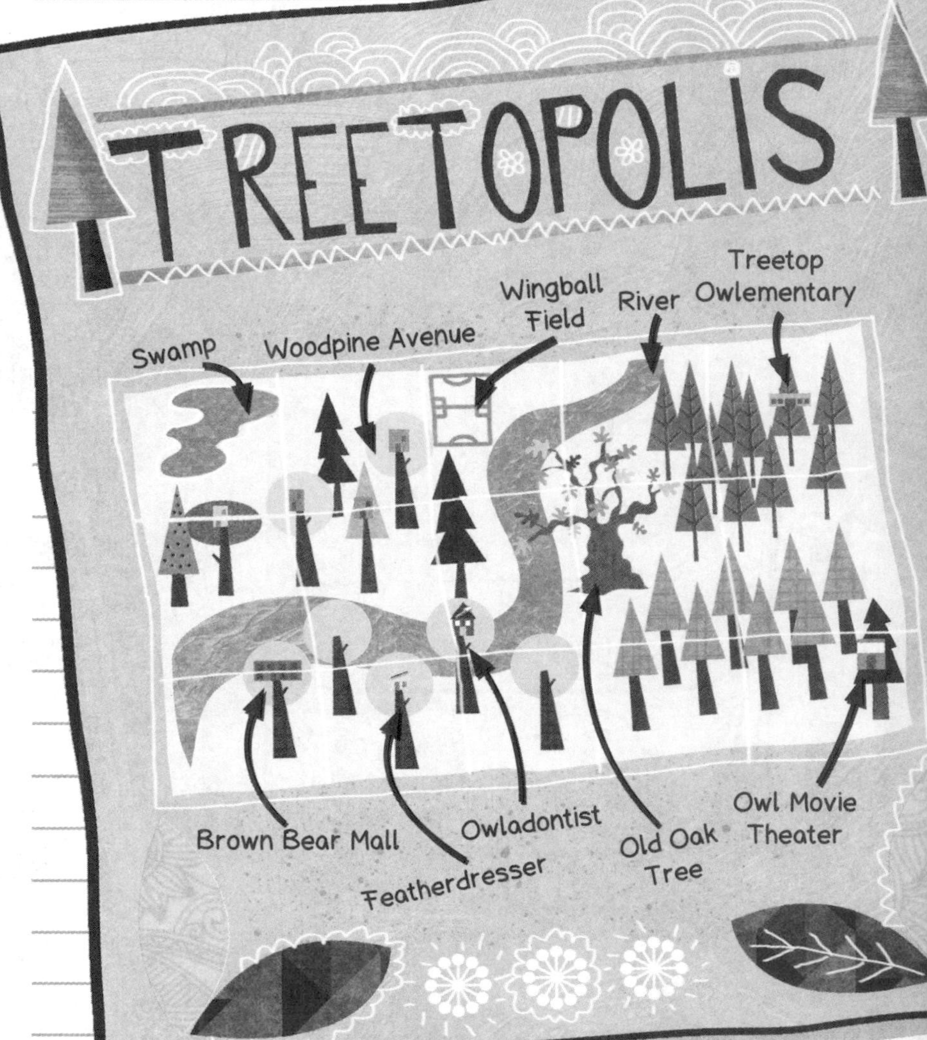
TREETOPOLIS
Swamp
Woodpine Avenue
Wingball Field
River
Treetop Owlementary
Brown Bear Mall
Featherdresser
Owladontist
Old Oak Tree
Owl Movie Theater

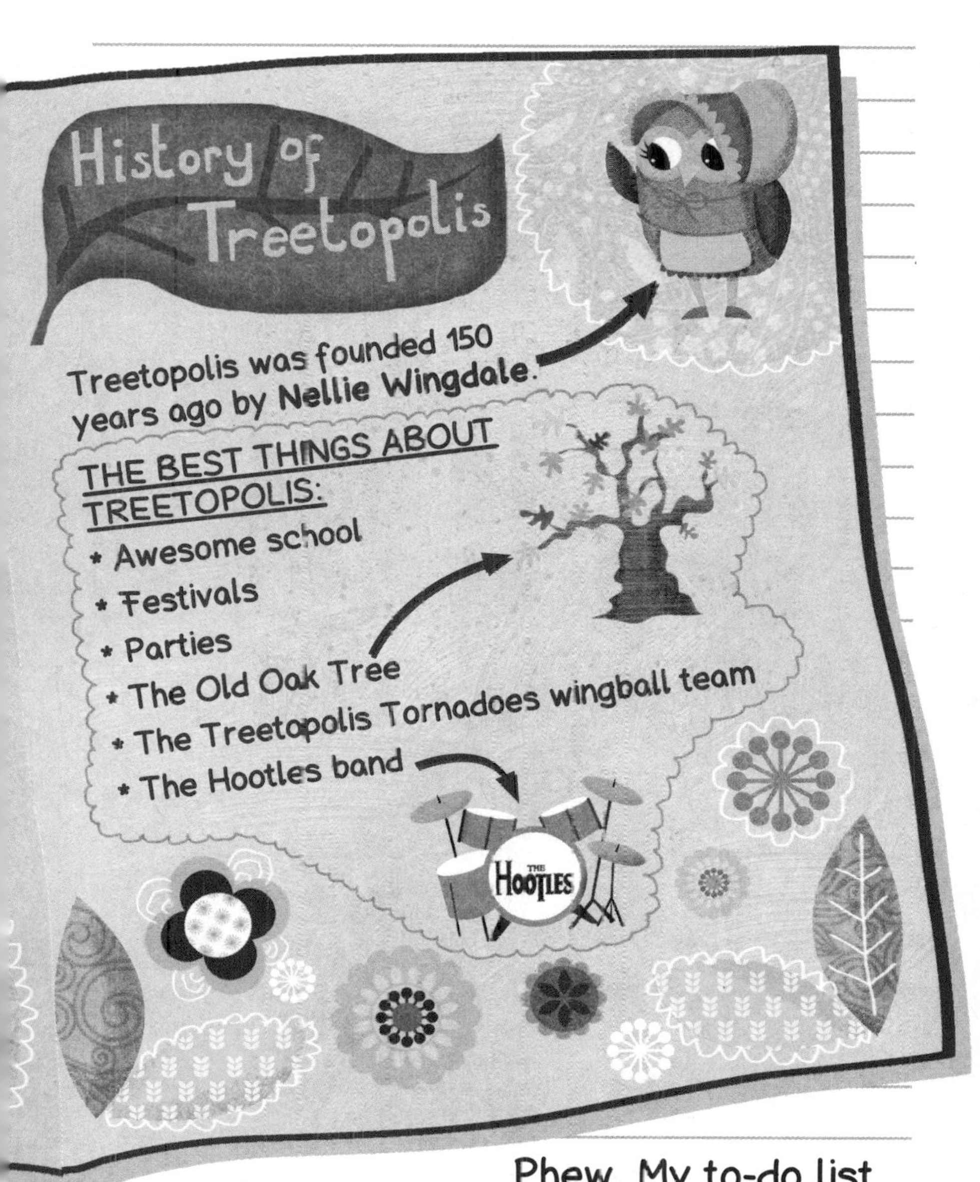
History of Treetopolis
Treetopolis was founded 150 years ago by Nellie Wingdale.
THE BEST THINGS ABOUT TREETOPOLIS:
* Awesome school
* Festivals
* Parties
* The Old Oak Tree
* The Treetopolis Tornadoes wingball team
* The Hootles band
THE HOOTLES

Phew. My to-do list is complete! Bedtime!

5

5 The New Owl

Monday

Lucy and I flew to school together.

Eva, my new puppet-show theater is so cool!
I can't wait to see it!

So, what did you make for the new owl?
I made Hailey a necklace and a guide to Treetopolis!
I'm sure she'll like them!
Quick – let's fly faster! I can't wait to meet her!

Lucy and I normally sit next to each other in class. But, Diary, I was just SO excited to meet the new owl!

Lucy, do you mind if I sit over there so Hailey can sit next to me? Sue told me she wants to be friends with Hailey, too . . . I just don't want Hailey to have to sit next to Sue.
Oh, okay.

I'm worried that Lucy felt a bit sad about me changing seats. But I didn't want Hailey to have to sit next to Meany McMeanerson on her first day.

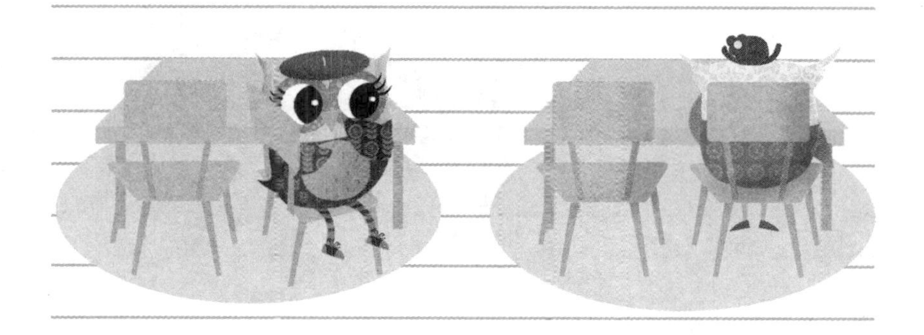

Then Hailey flew into the classroom!

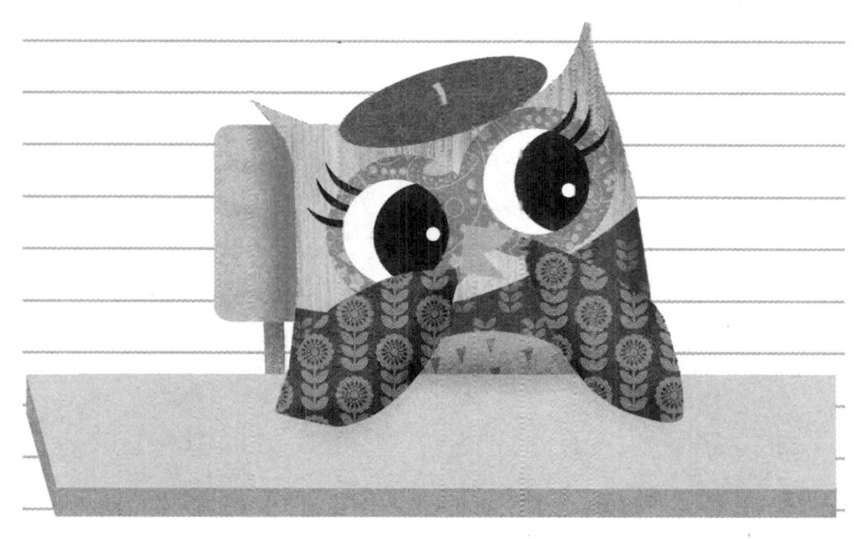

Class, I'd like you all to meet Hailey.
Hello.
Hailey, please sit wherever you'd like.

I waved my wings in the air and pointed at the empty seat next to me.

But I guess Hailey didn't see me because she sat next to Lucy instead. In my old seat.

We all turned in our forest drawings. Then Mrs. Featherbottom said Hailey could work on the crossword puzzle with Lucy.

I sat on my own and wrote my story about George's sister.

I planned to give Hailey the necklace and the guide after school. But things didn't go as planned.

I flew up to Hailey after school.

Hi, Hailey! I'm Eva.
Hi, Eva! Nice to meet you!
I made this necklace for you!
That's lovely! Thank you, Eva. I can't wear it this week though. I'm wearing a special necklace my dad gave me for my first week at the new school.
Oh. Okay.

I couldn't tell if Hailey really liked the necklace. She took it. But I felt silly as I flew away.

I decided not to give Hailey the guide until tomorrow. I want to look it over again, to make sure it looks really good. I hope she'll like it more than she liked the necklace. Sleep well, Diary.

It's All Going Wrong!

Tuesday

Hi Diary,

Lucy and I flew to school together. But we didn't say much. Do you think Lucy feels bad that Hailey sat next to her and not me?

School wasn't much better tonight. We worked on the newspaper, which was great. But Hailey sat next to Lucy again. The two of them were laughing like the best of friends.

I also saw Hailey talking with Sue.

I felt a bit sad. I still hoped that Hailey would want to be my friend, too. And I hoped my guide would make everything better.

I finally gave the guide to Hailey after school.

Hi, Hailey! I made this for you. It shows a map of Treetopolis. There's a list of places to visit and everything.
Wow, Eva! That's so sweet of you! But I already sort of know my way around. Sue gave me a tour.
Oh.
Your guide is pretty, though! I'd love to hang it up at home, if that's okay.

Oh, Diary! I just felt so silly! My cheeks went red.

I flew home as quickly as I could.

Mom knew I was upset. Moms always do. She gave me a warm cup of **BUG CHOCOLATE**, a hug, and some good advice.

You can't make friendships happen, Eva. You should always be yourself and hope that others like you for who you are.
I know, Mom. I just really want Hailey to like me.

It sounds like you girls may just need some time to get to know each other. Why don't you invite Hailey over for a sleepover on Saturday?
That's a great idea! Thanks, Mom!

Diary, I feel MUCH better. My plan for tomorrow: invite Hailey to sleep over!

Sleepover Disaster!

Wednesday

We all had fun working on the Owl Times in school tonight.

I finished writing the news story about George's sister Jenny.

Lucy and Hailey finished working on their crossword puzzle.

Zara kept taking pictures of EVERYONE all the time.

Zac reported the weather to us (whether we wanted to know it or not)!

Carlos drew funny cartoons of each of us.

Lilly wrote about our **WINGBALL** game for the sports page.

Jacob wrote about **OWLANDO** for the travel page. (His family went on vacation there.) And Sue wrote about what owls should and should not wear.

George designed the front page. And Macy checked everything for mistakes.

It was exciting to see our newspaper coming together!

After school, I flew up to Hailey.

Hi, Hailey!
Hi, Eva!
I wanted to see if, um, you maybe wanted to come over for a sleepover on Saturday.
That's really thoughtful of you, Eva! Thank you! But, well, I'm sorry – I've already agreed to sleep over at Lucy's this Saturday. Maybe you could ask Lucy if you can come, too?

I flew off before Hailey finished talking. I felt embarrassed. Again.

When I got home, I tried to cheer myself up. I dressed Baxter in a pink ballerina outfit. But then my brother, Humphrey, came into my room . . .

Who's ever heard of a "bat-erina"? Baxter looks so silly!
Oh, you're such a squirrel-head, Humphrey!

I wasn't having any fun without Lucy. So I called her.

Hi, Lucy.
Hi, Eva.
Just wondered what you were doing?
I'm busy, Eva.
Oh.
Well you've been busy this week, too.
Oh. I guess so.
Bye, Eva.

Diary, I think I may have lost my very best old friend by trying SO hard to make a new friend. Maybe Sue was right. Why would Hailey want to be friends with me? She only wants to be friends with cool owls, and Lucy is the coolest.

♡ And the Winner Is . . . ♡

Thursday

I flew to school all by myself tonight.

Principal Eggmington flew into our class. He came to tell us who had won the forest drawing contest.

All of your artwork was flaperrific! But I chose the most colorful drawing and the one that looked like it had taken the longest to make. The winner is . . .

I held my breath.

Eva Wingdale!
1ST

I won! I couldn't believe it! Everyone clapped as I flew up to collect my prize.

Now I have two tickets to see **WINGDERELLA** on Saturday!

movie pass
WINGDERELLA admit one
WINGDERELLA admit one

But Diary, I don't have a best friend to take with me anymore. It really looks like Hailey is Lucy's new best friend.

After school, all I wanted to do was hang out with Lucy. But I've really messed that up. So I made some new puppets instead.

Here's me and Lucy:

I even made little Baxter and Rex puppets.

I pretended I was playing with them in Lucy's new puppet-show theater. Puppet Eva and Puppet Lucy are best friends. I just wish the real Eva and Lucy were, too.

Humphrey saw me playing with the puppets. I thought he was going to make fun of me. But he didn't . . .

Eva, you have been moping around for ages. I'm bored of it. Why don't you just say sorry to Lucy?
Because I'm worried Lucy doesn't want to be my friend anymore. You see, I haven't been very nice to her this week. I didn't hang out with her. And I didn't sit next to her. Really, all I've talked about this week is the new owl.

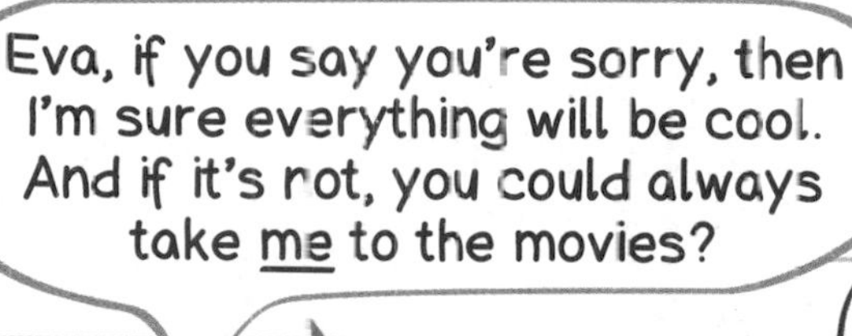
Eva, if you say you're sorry, then I'm sure everything will be cool. And if it's not, you could always take me to the movies?

Argh!! No way, Humphrey!!

Humphrey is right. (Not about my extra movie ticket!) I know what I need to do. Don't worry, Diary. I have a BIG plan to fix everything!

A BIG Sorry

Friday

I flew to school super early tonight, Diary. Mrs. Featherbottom was the only owl there.

Hello, Eva!
Has the Owl Times been printed yet?
Not yet. I was just about to print it. Why?

May I add something to it first?
Sure, Eva. Then maybe you could help me pass out the newspapers?
I'd love to help!

I placed a newspaper on each desk.

Everyone started reading as soon as they got to class!

The Owl Times

Owl Always Love You

BY EVA WINGDALE

I learned something big this week: friendship is tricky. When I tried to make a new friend, I nearly lost an old friend. My oldest, bestest friend – Lucy Beakman. Lucy always makes me happy, always has time for me, and always lends a helping wing when I need one. I know now that while it's great to make new friends, we must never forget how special our old friendships are. (Lucy, I'm so sorry. I miss you.)

Me and Lucy when we were baby owlets

Lucy looked up after she read the article. I flew over.

I'm sorry I haven't been a good friend, Lucy. I miss you.
I miss you, too, Eva!

You're the best friend ever!
No, you're the best friend ever!

I handed Lucy my movie tickets.

You and Hailey should go see Wingderella before your sleepover.
Thank you, Eva! But I want you to come to the sleepover, too! Besides, your drawing was amazing! I couldn't see Wingderella without you.

Hailey must have heard us talking. She flew right over.

What if the three of us chipped in to pay for a third ticket? Then we could all go!
That's a great idea!
That would be owlsome!

Just then, I realized another BIG thing about friendship: the more, the merrier!

Who else wants to come to the movies tomorrow?

Everyone raised their wings! Then Mrs. Featherbottom **HOOTED**:

Eva has perfect timing, class! Principal Eggmington said he was so impressed with your newspaper that we can all take a field trip to the movies!

Now everyone can go!

Sleepover Success!

Saturday

I flew over to Lucy's house as soon as I woke up tonight. I showed her the puppets I made.

I love them!

We put on a puppet show for Baxter and Rex! It was such a **HOOT**!

Then Hailey came over. The three of us chose outfits for the field trip. We all looked **FLAP-TASTIC**!!! Hailey even wore the necklace I gave her!

Thank you for this necklace and for the guide, Eva.
You're welcome, Hailey.

It's great to have new friends!
And it's great to have old friends!
Friends are flaperrific. Especially mine!

Here's a photo of ALL of us at the movies tonight. (Kiera came back from vacation just in time!)

Now I've got to run, Diary, or I'll be late for the sleepover with my newest and oldest best friends — Hailey and Lucy! See you next week!

OWL
DIARIES

How much do you know about Eva and the New Owl?

My class is excited to create the Owl Times! What are some of the newspaper jobs the owls have? Which job would you want?

Look at pages 268-269. What can you learn about Treetopolis from Eva's guide?

Reread pages 282-283. What advice does Eva's mom give her about friendships?

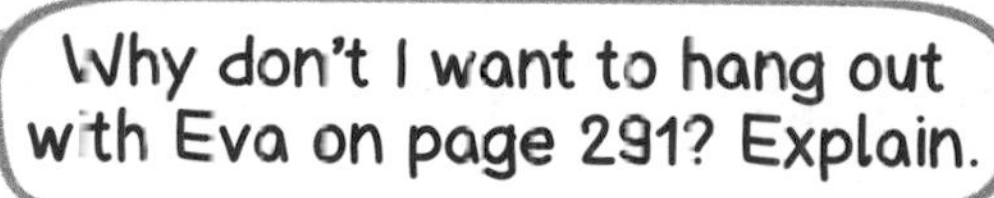
Why don't I want to hang out with Eva on page 291? Explain.

Write an article for the Owl Times about why your friends are important to you.

schclastic.com/branches

Rebecca Elliott was a lot like Eva when she was younger: She loved making things and hanging out with her best friends. Now that Rebecca is older, not much has changed — except that her best friends are her husband, Matthew, and their children. She still loves making things, like stories, cakes, music, and paintings. But as much as she and Eva have in common, Rebecca cannot fly or turn her head all the way around. No matter how hard she tries.

Rebecca is the author of JUST BECAUSE and MR. SUPER POOPY PANTS. OWL DIARIES is her first early chapter book series.

Read more OWL DIARIES books!
OWL DIARIES
Eva's Treetop Festival
1
OWL DIARIES
Eva Sees a Ghost
2
OWL DIARIES
A Woodland Wedding
3
OWL DIARIES
Eva and the New Owl
4
OWL DIARIES
Warm Hearts Day
5
OWL DIARIES
Baxter is Missing
6
OWL DIARIES
The Wildwood Bakery
7
OWL DIARIES
Eva and the Lost Pony
8
OWL DIARIES
Eva's Big Sleepover
9